Grace Manderfeld

Into the Forest

Into the Forest

GRACE MANDERFELD

ISBN 979-8-218-12766-4

For all of my family and friends who inspired, loved, and encouraged me along the way.

And especially for my Grandpa Rich and Grandma Barb, who helped me discover my passion for writing.

PROLOGUE

The old man was in possession of the map that led me on the wildest of adventures. His wrinkled but gentle hand reached out to me, the map inches away. My whole arm shook with anticipation, and the ripped, stained piece of paper felt warm between my fingertips when he handed it to me.

"My grandmother found that," the old man said from behind the counter of the small, run-down souvenir shop in the middle of a forest, somewhere in northern Minnesota. "Washed up inside a bottle on the shore of Camp Honey Bear." My eyes wandered across the page, following the little drops of dark brown ink. There were symbols scattered along the paper too, but it was hard to make out exactly what they were supposed to be.

"Camp Honey Bear? Could the other pieces of this map be washed up on shore too?" I asked, looking up into the man's big, blue eyes.

"You know, Lucas, if they are, *I* never found them after many years of searching. And if you do find them at Camp Honey Bear? Well, I'll be surprised!"

Chapter 1

Camp Honey Bear

Hannah

"Do I *really* have to go?" I ask from the car's back seat, aware that I'm already signed up and there's no escape now. There's this huge program going on like summer camp, and my aunt signed me up without asking me first. You have to be 11 to 16 years old to go to Camp Honey Bear, and I'm 15.

"Yes, you do. It's only for the summer, and I'm sure you'll make friends!" my Aunt Stacey says as she makes a left through the town, her car's blinker clicking.

"You know kids in my school say this camp is *haunted*, right?" I ask her, not truly believing this theory, but it's my last resort. I think of my classmates' whispers before summer break about how people have seen *shadows* of things that aren't really there…hidden away in the woods. Screams after midnight, but no source of the sound. Did these strange stories really happen at Camp Honey Bear? I wonder.

Aunt Stacey chuckles while she drives. "You have to know that ghost stories aren't true, Hannah. Besides, you'll be so busy having fun and making friends, you won't even think about those rumors."

"Okay, if you say so," I reply. I try to put the ghost stories out of my mind, but I've always been freaked out by scary movies. And thanks to those rumors, I'm starting to get a bad feeling about this summer camp.

I sigh deeply. On top of the possible ghosts, I start to feel the weight of going somewhere alone with no friends for support. I start to twirl my long, straight, brown hair around my fingers, making spirals that bounce right back to being straight again.

We pass the sign that reads *Wet Rock Shore*, that makes my going away official. Aunt Stacey and I moved to Wet Rock Shore a month ago, and she says this summer camp is a great way for me to make *friends*. The thing is…I'm very antisocial and shy around people I barely know. *Sarah and Izzy would make this unfortunate camp situation a lot easier.* They were my two best friends before we moved. I still call and text them, but it's not the same.

My aunt is a clothing designer, and she finally opened up her own store right under our apartment. We've moved five times so far, and every time it's been a huge change. For example, we used to live in loud, flashy New York City, and now we're living in a tiny town where everyone knows everyone. Because we move so much, as soon as I started fitting in at my old school, I had to change districts again.

We go to a very small school where 6th graders through 12th graders share the same building. I'm not too popular at my new school, but I'm fine with it and I'd like it to stay that way.

Ever since I was a baby, I've lived with Aunt Stacey. My parents passed away in a car crash when I was little. My dad was an only child, so there was no one left for me to live with. But luckily, my mom had a step-sister, Stacey. She always tells me about my parents though, like how my mom loved to paint and had curly, long hair. How my dad played piano and would tell the funniest jokes. Sometimes, I wonder what life would be like if they were alive. Then, I realize I have my aunt, and that makes me luckier than a lot of people.

While we roll away from town and onto the highway for the two-hour drive, I pull out my phone to text my two best friends, Izzy and Sarah, back in New York.

Me: Save me! I'm going to a summer camp in the woods! Kids in my school say that parts of the woods are haunted...and there have been sightings of ghosts.

Izzy: Ghosts? I doubt that's true, and besides it's going to be fine! I bet it'll be more fun than you think.

Sarah: Yeah, and you'll meet new people from Minnesota. Hopefully it's not true, but just in case, text us tomorrow! Maybe the ghosts will be nice anyway!

Me: Alright, you guys are too optimistic for this.

Sarah: :)

Izzy: Haha I gtg to gymnastics. Bye!

Sarah: Send us pictures Hannah! Bye!

I type goodbye and put my phone back in my bag. *I miss them. But as much as I do, I need to find new friends here.* For a while, I play a puzzle game on my phone, distracting myself.

Soon, my mind wanders, and I look out the window. All I see is endless trees and wildlife–until a big wooden sign comes up ahead. It reads:

Welcome Camp Honey Bear, come back next year!

"Earth to Hannah! We're almost there!" Aunt Stacey says.

Her voice surprises me, like someone slapped me in the face and said, *"Wake up Hannah! You're going to camp; accept it!"*

Aunt Stacey's car rolls past the sign and onto a bumpy forest trail surrounded by towering, hundred-year-old trees, then stops in a small, dirt parking lot.

Just then, I see something out the window: a short girl with bright, blonde hair comes out of a cabin. Her deep-brown eyes look worried, as if she's just done something she wasn't supposed to. I shift in my seat as the girl hovers there for a few seconds…and Aunt Stacy's voice makes me turn and glance at her instead.

"We're here!" she says cheerily.

I give her a smile and quickly look back, but the girl is gone. I turn my attention to the small crowd of people waiting for us on the sidewalk, log cabins and a lodge behind them. I watch tons of kids slowly exit the school buses, and others who arrive in cars like me. When I get out of the car with my duffel bag, I immediately feel the hot, fresh air dampen my skin.

I wave goodbye to Aunt Stacey as she's getting back in her car, and she mouths, "Try to make friends. Love you!" I give her a nod and smile, then swing my duffel bag over my shoulder and walk toward the buses and other campers.

An older woman with short, frizzy, gray hair walks out of a cabin. "Hello, kids! I know it's getting late, so we can go over camp rules in the morning. But we need to find our cabin counselors first! Now, I sent a list of numbers to your teachers and parents, and those numbers represent what cabin you will go to!"

Since Aunt Stacey told me, I already know I'm a Number Two, so I follow along the dirt and grass to the counselor with a giant *Two* taped to her shirt. A guy picking his nose budges in front of me to get to some other boys closeby. Gross! He's in my grade, 10th, and he's still this immature?

And of course, Bianca Dirkenson is standing only ten feet away from me. Bianca and her group of friends gave me a pretty "warm" welcome on my first day at this new school. Those girls made sure that when I tripped over my shoelaces and fell flat on my face, it was guaranteed to end up being recorded by all of them. Then they sent the video to all of Bianca's friends, which meant at least eight people willing to share it with *everyone* in the school. Ever since that embarrassment, I've been the laughing stock of Wet Rock Shore Junior School. Now, I tend to stay out of groups of people so no one notices me.

Bianca just *had* to go to Camp Honey Bear so she could post videos of her "roughing it." Oh please, we're going to be in cabins with air conditioning. That's definitely *not* what I'd call roughing it, I think.

As I stand at our cabin, trying to ignore Bianca, the counselor says, "Hi! I'm Michelle, and I'll be your cabin counselor! Feel free to just call me Michelle," she says. Her voice and personality almost knock me backwards! She's extremely chipper and very awake, even though the stars are coming out. "We're the Cardinal Cabin! So I'll give you a red T-shirt in the morning. Come on inside," she says, waving her hand toward our cabin with the red bird on it, which I assume is a cardinal. I haven't spent too much time outside–minus walking in Central Park and the one time Aunt Stacey took me to a state park to try kayaking–so I don't know birds very well.

We open the wood door with five other girls to find a well-kept, log cabin with a yellow and pink theme going for the walls, plus a white rug, little windows framed by curtains with pretty little flowers printed on them, and three bunk beds. I choose the bottom bunk of the bed closest to the door. There are two doors to the girls' bathroom and a storage closet tucked in the back of the room, separated with a big painting of a black bear. The bed sheets are pastel yellow with Camp Honey Bear printed on the center. We left our little town at 6 p.m., and it's almost 9:55 p.m. now. I yawn as Michelle says lights out in ten minutes in her cheery voice.

While we all unpack, get changed into our pajamas, start to make small talk, and some girls play a game, ten minutes pass by quickly, and Michelle walks into the cabin and flips the switch off on the wall. "Get some rest because tomorrow is when the fun starts!" Michelle says, then leaves us for the night.

I lay down on the mattress. It's not as hard as I expected it would be. When I close my eyes, I hear the other girls, Celia and Audrey, whispering above me. I've seen them in school, and they seem nice enough. But I wonder what they're whispering about.

Unlike Michelle, I don't think tomorrow is going to be very fun. I think I'm wasting my summer for this. Who am I turning into? An outdoorsy nerd?! Nope. I'm going to do the summer camp traditions, sure, but that doesn't mean I'm going to enjoy them.

I toss and turn for a while, but I can't fall asleep. Sitting up, I grab my phone from my bag hanging on the post of the bunk bed. I see Sarah and Izzy texted me, asking for a picture of camp, so I turn on flash mode and prepare to take a selfie to show them how boring camp is so far. But before I can take the picture, in my phone screen's reflection I see something carved into the wood on the head board behind me: *Catherine Whitlock and Susie Marvin 1955*.

As soon as I start to process the names, a drop of water slowly creeps down the wood, right over Catherine's name. I wipe the water away, thinking there must be some sort of crack in the ceiling. Sinking into my mattress, I start to pull the blankets over my head, but before I can, the window on the other side of the room fogs up...

I stare at the instantly foggy window. Weird. Suddenly two handprints appear on the glass…with no person behind the window, causing the shadows to come in the first place. I have to slap my hand over my mouth to cover the scream that started to leak out. A ghost? I think, my heart hammering hard. I look around to see if anyone saw what I just did, but everyone in my cabin is asleep. I take my hand off my mouth and force some deep breaths.

My mind starts racing, and the only thing I can think to do is run. *Run away from camp and never come back,* I tell myself. The thought fades quickly…because what if my mind is just messing with me? What if that was just a shadow in the dark, coming to life by the streaks of moonlight? Or some other kid playing a trick on us?

Suddenly, I do something very, very stupid. I climb out of bed, walk across the room and carefully open the door out into the dark, cool summer night. Closing the door softly, I feel a shiver run down my spine. My feet carry me all the way to the back of the cabin, where I can inspect the foggy window.

Tiptoeing, I look around to see if anyone is outside. A voice behind me makes me stumble over and fall flat on the ground, the grass is damp with water but there isn't a storm cloud in sight. My eyes drift upwards to see the same, short, blonde-haired girl I saw from the car earlier turning around to face me.

"I'll be fine; just go back to the cabin and *stay there,*" the strange girl says to me, her voice sounding reassuring but also a little scared.

Can she see me? I think, so terrified I'm shaking. I open my mouth to answer, but before I can, the girl standing in front of me glitches. Her whole body turns black and white, like an old movie, and slowly...she disappears.

My eyes grow wide as I lunge for the place the girl was just standing, grasping the air and *nothing* but the air. She's gone.

This cannot be possible, I think, carefully creaking open the door to the Cardinal Cabin. *I must be losing my mind*, I think. The small girl's frightened face burned into my memory. I quietly climb into my bunk, pull the blankets all the way up to my neck, and shut my eyes as tight as I can. This all has to be a dream.

CHAPTER 2

INVESTIGATING

Hannah

The good news is, I might know who Susie Marvin is! The bad news is…last night definitely wasn't a dream. The next morning, I blink away the sunlight and hop out of bed eagerly. I quickly put on shorts and a T-shirt in the bathroom and practically sprint outside. Running across the courtyard, I notice other kids are staring at me. Slowing down to a walk, I spot Ms. Marvin, the head of camp, standing outside the mess hall. Anyone can spot her frizzy, gray hair from a mile away.

On my way over to her, I muster up enough courage to make a detour behind my cabin, only to find something I regret. Footprints everywhere. And they aren't mine. Leading in the exact direction the girl was running. The footprints stop right where she disappeared. I shake off the feeling that someone is watching me, someone who is not a *camper* or *counselor*, and head over to Ms. Marvin.

When I reach her, I start to ramble, "Hi, Ms. Marvin I…" In the middle of my sentence the question slips out of my mouth, "What's your first name?"

Susie. "Susan," she replies, squinting her eyes and looking confused.

"Ok. Um, did you by any chance know someone named Catherine Whitlock?" I ask.

Her face turns quickly from confused to sentimental. "Well, believe it or not, I used to be a camper here when I was your age, and so was my best friend Cathy. We made so many good memories here; we even carved our names into one of the bunk beds in Cardinal Cabin." That explains that mystery, I think.

Ms. Marvin's face falls and she looks at the ground, "But one night, Cathy got a little too curious. All of the counselors threw a party deep in the forest to celebrate the Fourth of July…after all of us campers went to bed. I told her not to go because it's dangerous and she could get into lots of trouble." She takes a deep breath as we walk through the mess hall's entrance.

She leads me in silence over to a big wall with dozens of photographs hanging over the round lunch tables. She stops in front of one in particular, an old, framed, black and white newspaper clipping.

In the photograph, two girls around my age stand in front of the lake with canoe paddles in their hands. The girl on the left is slightly taller with dark, frizzy braided hair and a striped shirt. The girl on the right is shorter with the familiar bright blonde hair, freckles and a bucket hat.

The newspaper scrap reads:

Missing Girl - Catherine Whitlock last seen on Friday, July 4, 1955, 11:40 p.m. If found, please call her parents and Camp Honey Bear immediately.

It lists the phone numbers underneath, and there is also a short article about Catherine and her disappearance.

"Cathy is the one on the right with the bucket hat." Ms. Marvin shakes her head. "She didn't listen to me. She ran off, and I tried to go after her, but she kept telling me she was fine. After all, we *were* almost twelve, she said. The next morning, the counselors said she never showed up at the party. And she was nowhere to be seen. We looked everywhere in the woods and at camp. The police couldn't find her either." Her eyes turn misty for a second. "I miss her so much to this day. I always wonder…what happened to her?"

I say sadly, "I'm so sorry." I can't imagine my best friend–like Sarah or Izzy–just vanishing, going missing and never being found.

CHAPTER 3

THE WILDERNESS

Oliver

"Oh gosh, oh gosh, oh gosh, oh gosh," I repeat under my breath, feeling uneasy about this *Camp Honey Bear.* I mean, I've never liked the woods anyway. There are so many germs and unsafe things. Like for example, *what if I drown in the lake? What if I get eaten by a bear? What if I lose my pouch in the woods? And most importantly, what if I get LOST??? I'm only 13!*

How will I make it through the entire summer if I already know there's a long list of things to be afraid of? I wonder. Even the rumors in school scare me about camp. Some people say a ghost girl haunts the camp. Some of my classmates who have been to this camp before swear they've seen her ghost. *What if ghosts ARE real?* I think, adding this fear to my growing list.

"Alright O-dog, let's get going!" my older brother, Brandon, says in his deep, cool voice. He's the captain of the football team and even wore his designer sunglasses. Why can't I be like him? Well, maybe it's because I'm very UNCOOL in many ways. I definitely don't play sports. Instead, I spend my time doing math equations and science experiments, using my sewing kit, and reading nonfiction textbooks.

Brandon's sports car starts up, and off we go. I buckle my seatbelt for safety while nauseously looking at my house as it gets farther and farther away. I get extremely homesick easily. I'm going to miss my warm, quilted bed, the bookshelves with my textbooks, and the backyard where I host my bird watching club.

Brandon is one of the camp counselors, so I have to learn how to be a *junior* counselor. Of course, I don't want to drive hours to a place where kids my age learn how to survive in the wilderness, play camp games, build shelters, and go canoeing. I'm not that type of guy.

I'd rather be at the Prominent Science Camp that started yesterday. I bet the lucky kids there are already learning how to use a telescope or a microscope…or something with the word "scope" in it! I would do anything to be learning amazing facts at that Science camp instead.

"Hey little bro, you wanna get a burger at McDonald's?" Brandon asks me.

I tell him that would be great. "Only three hours to go!" I add, watching our little car icon on the roads of the GPS screen. I got this GPS system for Christmas, and I've been waiting for the chance to use it. Despite the GPS excitement, I imagine what camp is going to be like when we arrive.

I'm really hoping I won't be in a cabin with all of the jocks. They'll make fun of me the first chance they get. Even *I* would make fun of me.

"Hello, welcome to McDonald's. What can I get for you?" one of the employees says from the microphone inside of the menu.

"Umm, I'll get two Big Macs with a side of fries and two large strawberry milkshakes please," Brandon tells the female voice in the box. He's ordering the milkshakes just to sweeten me up, I think. He knows I'm not the outdoorsy type, but our parents and Brandon think camp is a "valuable experience."

The burgers were fine I guess, and I liked the sweet milkshake, but I can't get my mind off Camp Honey Bear. I'm a junior counselor, and eventually I'll have to take Brandon's place as head counselor. All this is making me sick. But maybe I'll enjoy it? Maybe they'll have some activities about experimenting, like we would in Science class? And the S'mores are always a plus. You never know. At least Brandon will be there to help me, I think, trying to calm myself down.

I shift in my seat, anxiously awaiting camp. Brandon thinks it's going to be fun, but I don't. I mean, as far as I can tell, I won't have any friends there, so that makes things more difficult. I polish my glasses with my shirt, making sure they are in pristine shape for when I arrive.

The smell of fast food hangs in the car as I glance at my GPS, then out the window. Trees fly by before I can get a good look at them to estimate their age.

"Hey, what's up?" Brandon asks, looking at me through the mirror above him.

"It's nothing," I say quietly, looking at my hands.

"Come on, you've been acting weird all day. Are you sick?"

"No! No, it's not like that at all!" I reply, a bit too frantically.

"Then what is it?" His face looks too sympathetic for me not to answer.

"I, um. I'm really nervous about camp. You know me. I hate dangerously mysterious things like the forest." I cringe at how nerdy I sound. "Besides, I don't really know anybody there."

"Oliver, there's nothing to be afraid of! And you know me! I'll be there," he says with a smile. "You'll meet new people too, and you might even find your first girlfriend! Camp is a great place to meet cute girls." Brandon raises his eyebrows.

If I was cool like you, girls might like me, I think. "Yeah, I guess. Thanks," I say to my brother. This could either turn out to be the best summer ever or the worst. I guess I'll find out soon.

CHAPTER 4

A NIGHT ALONE

Audrey

I'm definitely a perfectionist. And a leader. At only 14 years old, I'm the leader of the school's Recycling Club, the co-captain of the Swim Team, and the head of the Girls' Archery Team. Let's just say if I was put in a movie, I'd be the main character no doubt.

I've been psyched up for the past few days because I'm going to camp! *This is my time to shine. To show everybody that I'm a born leader.* Still, I'm most excited to go to camp to make friends. I don't have many friends. All of my past friends said that I'm bossy, but I like to think of my bossiness as leadership. *I'm going to keep this camp together, starting tomorrow night when I board the bus.*

*****

That bus ride was boring! Mostly because I sat alone. When we *finally* arrive, I see five cabins. To sort them, we use numbers. I'm a Number Two, so I walk over to the lady wearing a Two shirt and ask her where our cabin is. She says her name is Michelle and she'll be our head counselor. A few other kids come off of the bus and walk over to her as well. She seems very excited to see all of us and it shows in her high, bubbly voice.

Michelle leads us over to a cabin with a red cardinal on the door. All the girls in my group take their time and stay behind me. *Good.* When Michelle opens the wooden door, I'm very surprised to see the colors pink and yellow! Since almost everything is wood and logs here, I was expecting more brown. Instead, there are cute little flowers everywhere and lots of space for us to put our clothes. "You girls get settled in. I'll come back to check on you soon," Michelle says. Everyone decides on their bed, and soon we're getting ready to go to sleep.

I grab my pajamas and head to the girl's bathroom. It's an all girls' cabin, so I don't know why they bothered writing *Girls* on the door. In fact, all the cabins are boys or girls, not mixed. When I finish putting on my soft gray sweatpants and white shirt, I step back out to find the other girls bonding. They're sitting cross-legged on the floor and chatting.

"Audrey! We're playing a get to know you game. Do you wanna play?" Kim asks, sliding up her glasses on her nose.

"Sure! How does the game work?" I ask, sitting down in the middle of Bianca and Kim, who seem to have an invisible yardstick between them, and Bianca's holding it. I scoot a bit closer to Kim because I can already tell she's much nicer than Bianca.

"It's called Two Lies and a Truth. You have to say one thing about yourself that's true and two things that aren't true. Then you have to guess the truth. Here, I'll start." Kim looks up like she's thinking. *So basically two truths and a lie backwards?* I think. Kim says, "I'm severely allergic to cats, I don't like reading, and my favorite hairstyle is a ponytail."

I can tell which one is the truth by the way she wears her hair everyday at school, but I don't want her to think that I just want to win every game, so I tell one of the lies instead, "The truth is that you hate reading!"

"No, silly, I love reading! The truth was that my favorite hairstyle is a ponytail!" she says, and I almost burst out laughing.

"No duh, Kim. You had your hair in a ponytail until we got ready for bed," Bianca grumbles, clicking through Snapchats on her phone. She's barely paying attention to our game.

Kim makes a face at Bianca, then seems to brush away her comment. She pushes up her glasses again. "You can go next if you want," she says to me. The other girls, besides Bianca, nod.

I scowl at Bianca. "Are you playing or not?" I point at the phone in her hand, since she's still not paying attention.

She sighs dramatically. "I'm listening. God, calm down," Bianca says, eyes still on her phone's screen.

"If you want to play, then put your phone away now." My bossy side is coming out, but I don't care. Kim smirks. Bianca glares at me, and I glare back until she sets her phone face down in her lap. "Okay, let me think," I say, forming my two lies and one truth in my head.

After my turn, I realize that Hannah didn't want to play the game. Well, neither did Bianca but *still*. I glance up at Hannah laying on her stomach in the bottom bunk. She's on her phone, texting someone it looks like. I assume she's saying goodnight to her mom, and that reminds me to text mine before bed. I pull out my phone from my pocket and text *I love you, goodnight* to my mom. I hit send, and just then Michelle walks into our cabin and says lights out.

*****

I wake up the next morning to a really strong smell. Glue? Mixed with–rubber? I climb down the bunk's ladder and put my crazy curly hair up in a bun. Nobody's in the cabin, so I waver on tired legs outside. I'm not a morning person.

The log cabins sit in a circle around the central square, all dirt and grass, not even tar. The birds and grasshoppers are chirping in the hot morning sun. Luckily, the trees give shade.

Michelle, Kim, Celia, new girl Hannah, Bianca, and another girl who I haven't seen yet are standing in the courtyard. They're all at a wooden picnic table with gloves on.

"Think fast!" Celia says, tossing a pair of rubber gloves to me. I obviously caught them because I was in softball last summer.

"What are you guys doing?" I ask, putting the gloves on.

"We're making some decorations for our cabin!" Michelle explains. I nod, looking at the other cabin counselors and campers dragging tables out into the yard. One girl drops all of her craft glitter and is now completely covered in pink sparkles. Luckily, she was all the way on the other side of the courtyard. Pink isn't my best color.

I walk up to our table and ask what the heck we're making. Hannah explains that we're taking blown up balloons and wrapping sticky glue and water covered yarn around them. And then when the yarn is dry, we pop the balloons, put lights inside, and then we have hollow yarn lanterns.

I grab a balloon and start wrapping it in the glue covered yarn. It's sticky, but fun! kind of like my old Girl Scouts and Environmental Club. I quit both of them because no one liked me. I first learned to shoot a bow and arrow in Girl Scouts though, and I still practice my archery in my backyard and on the school team. It's more of a hobby. I'm pretty good at it though!

We spend at least an hour making our yarn lanterns, talking and laughing as Michelle leads the conversation to get to know us all better. I'm happy with my yarn lantern, but my fingers feel caked with the super sticky glue. I can't help but feel sticky the whole rest of the day, and I wonder what else will stick with me from this camp.

*****

Later that evening, after our crafts and a tour of the camp, I walk down to the archery range by a pond in the opposite direction of the lake. Good thing I brought my bow and arrow to camp!

Fireflies surround the clear, shallow water. Instead of focusing on the targets for practice, I draw back my bowstring and aim my practice arrow at the little flashing sunfish swimming in the water. As expected, I miss because they swim away like lightning. My arrows land in the mud and rocks with splashes, and I don't mind. This is one thing that I enjoy more than others at camp: being alone with nature.

The sun goes down at nine o'clock, and I march back up to the big circle of shadowed cabins in the bright, orange and pink sunset. The door of the Cardinal Cabin creaks open, and a pillow strikes me in the face. At least it's soft and full of feathers. A few of the boys from Otter Cabin are hanging out in our cabin until curfew.

"Sorry!" Celia yells from across the room.

Hannah is on her bunk again. Watching. Observing.

Celia whacks Oliver with a pillow, and he only smiles dreamily. I can tell he has a little crush on Celia. She doesn't seem to notice though. I look up at the lanterns we made earlier, which Michelle hung up on the ceiling. They sure do look beautiful, I think, as the enchanting, yellow glow spreads throughout our room.

CHAPTER 5

THE LAKE

Oliver

It's all ok so far. I'm talking about Camp Honey Bear. So *far.*
That means something bad could happen any time now. At least I can
see at night now in the cabin, thanks to our homemade lanterns.
They're pretty strict about lights out; I know this from the junior
counselor training and Brandon. No night lights are even allowed, but
the lanterns are great. Now I'll be able to see any danger that comes
my way. Like if a bear breaks into the cabin, I'll be ready to play
dead.

Being a junior counselor and all, I need to be prepared for
anything. I don't have any real duties yet because I'm technically still
in training, but practice makes close to perfect.

I open my big book titled *Survival Tips for the Wild.* The first
chapter describes how to use matches. The second chapter is about
what to do if your tent gets infested with INSECTS–one of my
biggest concerns about this place. One time, when I was camping out
on my screen porch, Brandon left the door open, so I woke up to
mosquito bites all over me! Ever since that experience, I have lost any
interest in studying or even reading about bugs.

"Put away your nerdy book. You're gonna miss canoeing," Lucas says to me as he walks into the cabin. He has his swim trunks on and grabs a paddle from the barrel in the corner.

I really *don't* want to go canoeing. My first thought is of *sharks.* Then I realize this is Minnesota. There aren't any sharks. Especially not in a lake. Well in that case...

"Ok, I'm coming!" I say to Lucas, but then realize he left the cabin a while ago. Great. I'm talking to no one.

I reach for my bathing suit from my suitcase. Dang it! My mom packed my ducky suit! Oh no. I'm a dead fish. Dead fish? Now *they* are in Minnesota. What if I find one in the lake?! Eww! No no no no no!

I put on the embarrassing swim trunks and take off my glasses, putting them safely on my nightstand. Then I walk down to the lake on a dirt path framed with wildflowers. When I arrive on the sandy shore, the panic kicks in. Lakes are filthy with all sorts of gross things. I think back to what Brandon told me in the car and hold my head an inch higher, hoping none of the girls see my ducky trunks.

Michelle waves from the Lifeguard chair, and I give a cautious wave back. I can sense the eyes of other kids turn to me as the smell of sunscreen and sand fills my lungs. They see my ducky swimsuit…with the rubber ducks all over it. But there's no turning back now!

Ok, one foot in front of the other, one foot...arghhhh! I scream so loud, most of the seagulls and other birds fly off. Michelle runs down from the lifeguard station, looking concerned. "I think something bit me!" I yell. I turn around looking for Brandon; he would know what to do in case of a sea creature crisis.

Michelle scopes out the waters for any sign of a predator. "Nope, just those little minnows swimming. Probably thought your toes were fish food," Michelle explains. With her every word, my face gets redder. How could I mistake a scary fish or snapping turtle for an inch-sized minnow? Stupid, stupid, stupid. I hear Lucas laughing from one of the canoes out on the water.

I wish Brandon was here, I think. He'd defend me and make me feel better, probably teach me how to canoe like it was as easy as finding bacteria under a microscope. He's busy leading his campers though, and we'll meet up for dinner in the mess hall later like usual.

I have to prove to Lucas that I can be fearless too. I just have to figure out how. How can people like to just kayak out to the middle of the lake and not have a care in the world? I hurry into the boys' bathhouse, pondering a heroic move I can make so everyone will just forget about the minnows incident. I wipe my sandy, wet feet off on the bathhouse's rug.

Once I'm done showering and back in the cabin, I come up with a list in my journal I brought from home. I scribble with my favorite, ballpoint pen. First idea to be heroic and cool: I successfully build a shelter when we have the shelter building competition. Second option: I go into the woods and gather cross rocks for my fellow campers. Cross rocks are a natural phenomenon usually found in water. It looks like there's little crosses carved into them. Well, obviously I have to paddle one of the canoes to find them. I can't risk getting bit by another minnow…or something bigger. My last option is the scariest: wait for night, then rustle off any dangerous animal that comes out after dark. Yeahhh…not the last one. Waaaaaayyy too dangerous.

*****

The next morning, with my list in mind, we are called outside by the camp owner, Ms. Marvin, for another activity. She walks up to the crowd of kids anxiously waiting. "Okay campers, time for the shelter building contest! You are allowed to find sticks and other materials in the woods, but you are strictly forbidden to go past the gate. The gate is what protects the camp from any dangerous animals or other things. We wouldn't want any of you to get lost." Ms. Marvin looks down at the ground, and then snaps out of it. "The gate is about a half mile out. Find teams of three to eight people, and let's get started!"

Okiedokey, this should be easy, I think, walking up to Celia, who is the prettiest girl I've ever seen. As I approach her, my palms start to sweat. "Hi Celia, d-do you want to be partners for the shelter building contest?" I'm stuttering a bit.

"Sure!" she replies. "But we need at least one more person."

"Ok, let's see if Audrey has a team?" I suggest.

CHAPTER 6

GO WITH THE FLOW

Kim

Oh. My. Gosh. Something unbelievable happened. *Lucas* just asked me to be on his team for the shelter building contest! I've had a major crush on him since the first day of camp, and boy is he cute. He has dark curly hair and amazing, cocoa-brown eyes.

Well, I'm only 13, and Lucas is 16, so I'm a little young for him. Lucas is funny and brave and cute. Did I already say totally in my league? Not really, but this is a dream come true! He couldn't even remember my name at first but now...I'm going to make the absolute best of this day! I don't know how this happened, but the universe is definitely calling me to him.

"Ok everyone, I'm gonna be looking for help with something...so just raise your hand if you'll be a good help!" Lucas says in a leader kind of tone. I push my glasses, then raise my hand.

But Bianca blurts, "What is this? School?! Aren't we supposed to be building a shelter?" She has always been mean. Not only to me either! To poor Hannah last month. Oh gosh. Bianca filmed Hannah when she tripped at school and sent it to everyone in her squad. One of the girls, Zoey I think, even sent it to ME on Snapchat! The surprising part is that no one sends me *anything ever.*

Other than my family, like my grandma. Hannah's been really embarrassed ever since. I feel bad for her. Oh well.

Lucas says something to me, but I'm still lost in thought. "I said, you can put your hand down!" he says, louder than before.

"Totally," I say, a little embarrassed.

"So we want our shelter to be awesome. We're going to split up. Three of us will collect sticks and other supplies we'll need. The other two of us will stay here and start building the base of the shelter by digging in the dirt and forming a hole," Lucas says.

I cross my fingers that I'm in his group. Lucas starts to drag people out into the woods. I'm one of those people! The leaves shade us, and I can almost taste the air getting fresher, now that there is no constant smokey smell from the nightly campfires. Bianca groans loudly. Then she whips her ponytail in Lucas's face...on accident, I hope.

"Let's get started!" Lucas says confidently. Apparently, I'm in the group of three, so I have to gather sticks with Lucas and Bianca! This is devastating and the best day ever at the same time! Devastating because Bianca is here, but incredible that I'm in the same forest as Lucas! Bianca pulls out her phone and starts texting. "Welcome to Lucas's mansion!" Lucas says, pointing down at a teeny tiny stick teepee.

"Like anyone bigger than an ant can fit in that thing!" Bianca scoffs, still speed texting.

"I think it's a great blueprint for a bigger version!" I exclaim. "Maybe Bianca and I can start gathering sticks, and then we can carry them back to the other teammates," I add, gathering sticks along the side of the forest. Only he shakes his head and says we have other plans.

"Other plans?" I ask. I'm confused. What does Lucas mean? We're supposed to be building a shelter.

He thinks for a second and then sticks a flower on top of Lucas's mansion. "Plans to explore and find the best shelter-making materials!" he says.

In that case, I suggest we go farther into the woods. "That's not a bad idea, Kimmy!" Lucas says.

He called me KIMMY! It's basically a pet name! Score. "Thanks," I say, blushing.

"Yeah, let's go past the gate!" he yells to us. "The fence that holds back danger," Lucas says in a whisper. "The fence that holds back treasure," he mutters as he walks ahead.

"I'm not getting in trouble for something that *dumb and deadly.* Why would you even want to go past the gate?!" Bianca shrieks, extending her neck to look for something in the distance. "Put it here please!" she yells to what seems to be no one at all.

But then a short boy with freckles and glasses runs through a giant bush behind me. I jump as he heaves a pink chair and mini cooler the size of my head over to Bianca. He sets it down carefully. "When I text you again, you can bring these things back to my cabin!" she yells to the boy, but he's already shuffling away. "Bye, nerd!" Bianca adds as she sits down on her chair. "You two can go past the disgusting gate, but I'm not risking getting killed by a bear–*or worse, chipping a nail!*" Bianca says. She opens the cooler and takes out a bottle of iced tea.

"Ok fine, stay here, but Kim and I are going past the gate," Lucas says.

"We are?!" I ask, sliding up my glasses, a habit I do when I'm nervous.

"Yup. You said you'd be a big help, so let's go." He grabs my hand and pulls me toward the north end of the woods.

"Okay," I mumble, liking this already. Bianca shouts something to us about getting killed. We walk through the woods for a little while. Then Lucas takes a left, and I follow, a bit nervous.

As we walk, I stare at the towering trees and watch two puffy-tailed squirrels chase each other. But my foot hits a root, and I trip. "Ouch!" I fall onto the ground and rub my back. I must've fallen on a rock or something. My glasses are missing, so my sight is all blurry now. I look around for my glasses. As I slip them back on, I realize I didn't fall on a rock. I fell on a *girl*.

"Watch where you're going," she says. She glares at me for a second, then pulls out a camera as she stands up. "Hey guys!

Welcome back to my YouTube live stream. Today, we are here at Camp Honey Bear! I know, how awesome is that?!"

I stare at her, and she presses the off button on her camera. At this point, Lucas has turned around from his trekking, spotting me in the dirt, leaves, and mushrooms, and his eyes get larger when he sees this video girl.

"Oh my goodness! I'm so sorry about that," the girl says to me in a fake voice. As Lucas gets closer, she offers her hand to him. He smiles and takes it. "Hey, you're Lucas from Otter cabin, right?"

I stand up, shaking dirt off of my hands. Sure, give your hand to Lucas, but don't help me up, I think.

"Yup. What are you filming for?" he asks.

"I have a YouTube channel. I figured I'd bring it to camp and get some exciting footage, but so far it's been really boring," Celia says sadly. This girl is definitely beautiful, even when she's sad, with long eyelashes framing her hazel eyes and shiny lip gloss highlighting her makeup.

"Maybe you could get some footage from beyond the gate!" Lucas suggests, looking at her perfect outfit and hair. She has long, golden blonde hair. And she's wearing a black and white plaid romper with cute, hightop white shoes, which are getting some grass stains from the wet ground. My cargo shorts and camp T-shirt are nothing compared to her outfit.

"Beyond the gate?" Celia asks. We continue hiking for a while. "So, I never got your name," Celia says, turning backwards and facing me. Of course, she's walking close to Lucas.

"Oh right. I'm Kim. But Lucas likes to call me Kimmy," I say, trying to make it sound as if he likes me.

"Ok, *Kimmy*." She turns to look at Lucas. "Is that right?" she asks sharply.

"Kimmy's a good nickname. But I'm one hundred percent single," Lucas says, and my heart sinks. He could tell I was trying to imply we were maybe, possibly a thing.

"Me too!" Celia says, and I slow down my walk so I can't hear them flirting. I hear rustling in the leaves behind me, and I turn around, thinking it might be a wolf, bear, skunk, possum, or any of the animals the counselors warned us about. A deer or bunny would be fine though, I think. Oh right, I'm not past the gate yet. We're safe until then.

"Don't touch me!" I hear a girl's voice ring out.

"Sorry, sorry," replies a boy's voice. Two other campers emerge out of the bushes. I recognize them as Audrey and Oliver.

"Hey guys. What are you doing here?" I ask.

"Oh hi," Oliver says timidly.

"Hey Kim!" Audrey says. "Let's go, Cardinal Cabin!"

"Yeah," I say, feeling nice to be remembered, Audrey starts to explain how Oliver and her wound up here. They say they were looking for Celia. Apparently, she disappeared right after the shelter building contest started...with her camera.

"Oh! She's up ahead with Lucas," I say, trying so hard for my voice not to crack.

"Hey Celia, where did you go?" Audrey shouts, echoing through the trees and long grass.

Celia runs over and apologizes, "Sorry I ran off. I had to find a signal to upload my videos. I absolutely *have to* keep my followers posted," she explains. Then she runs back up to Lucas.

Ever since we met Celia, my chances with Lucas are getting slimmer. "Guys, I think we found the gate!" Lucas shouts from up ahead. Celia's scream catches me off guard, and Oliver scurries to hide behind Audrey. What just happened?

CHAPTER 7

BEYOND THE GATE

Lucas

"Are you okay?" I ask Celia.

"Yeah I think so," she replies wearily, standing up. "My bracelet touched the fence, and it shocked me really hard."

"Oh, I thought I heard the head counselor say something about the gate before. It has a light electric shock, but I don't think it's too harmful if your bracelet only touched it," I tell her.

"Alright, so how are we supposed to get past the fence? I definitely got shocked when I touched it," Celia says, rubbing her wrist.

"Ok, just have to connect the A wire to the B wire then flip the switch and...we're in," Kim says, then closes the latch on the control panel. How could I have missed the control panel? The fence had a small, silver control box about 20 feet to our right. It can shut off the electrical shock! Everyone looks at Kim like she's got three eyes.

"What? I took robotics last year," she says casually. Immediately, Oliver walks over to her and starts talking about science.

"Now we need to climb the fence!" I say, stepping up onto the wire.

"Yeaahhh, I'm not so sure about climbing that tall of a fence and then jumping down from it," Celia says. She pulls her phone out of her pocket and uploads her latest videos.

"C'mon! It's only about nine feet high," I say, starting to inch my way to the top when...*Craaack!* I slide down to the bottom and land on my stomach. Ouch! The wind is knocked out of me.

"*Only* about nine feet, huh?" Celia asks, looking down at me. She reaches inside her hand purse and takes out her camera again. She flips it on and says, "Hey guys! Today I'm asking all of my followers to comment below on how we're supposed to get up this slippery ten foot fence! If we get to the other side, I'll live stream the whole adventure! Ok byeeee!" She flips the camera shut and says, "That's how you solve a problem."

I look at her, shake my head, and say, "I admire your enthusiasm, but we're not taking advice from a bunch of internet people."

"Fine, then I'll explore the great unknown by myself!" Celia says, walking a few steps in the direction we came.

Kim walks over, and I notice she has freckles, green eyes framed with rose gold glasses and light reddish brown hair pulled back in a low ponytail. She asks, "What's the plan?"

"I dunno, wherever the wind takes us I guess," I reply.

Audrey stomps over, apparently eavesdropping on us, and says, "That's *not* a plan!"

Kim tries, "Maybe we could find a rope or vine to climb?" She sounds quieter than before.

"Ehh, there's no vines or ropes anywhere," I say.

"Ok, so we have two hundred responses so far–actually two hundred twenty now!" Celia announces, holding her phone to each of our faces. I look closer and notice answers are flying in like crazy, two hundred ninety nine, three hundred, three hundred ten!

I reply, "I take it back. Maybe we could use some answers." *I need answers.* For my treasure that I've been trying to find for the past year. Do you think I came to this camp to row canoes or compete in camp games or to even make friends? Well yes. But not only those things! The main reason I came was to find my *treasure*. And that's what I'm planning to do.

CHAPTER 8

LEAVING

Hannah

I sit on my bunk, listening to the kids yelling and talking and laughing outside. I don't need to attract attention. I don't, after Bianca's bullying all over again. Yesterday, she got a video of me stepping in a pile of deer poop. It's like she can sense my every mistake! Then again, I can't stay in my cabin forever; I'll have to get outside eventually. I like chilling alone though. Maybe, I'll go outside for a bit, just until the shelter building contest ends. I don't want to join a shelter contest team in case I make another mistake, and I'm lucky no counselors noticed my absence.

I grab my light blue sweatshirt on the way out. Never know how camp weather will be! As I step outside, the humidity hits me like a sledgehammer. If there wasn't a breeze, I bet I would die from the heat. My sweatshirt isn't needed.

I think I heard the Head Counselor say something about the trail in the woods leading to the gate. Maybe if I follow it, I could catch a bus and get out of camp. I've had enough of this camp. There's no reason to stay. With Bianca bullying me and the girl I saw the first night…which I still shiver to think about…I need to leave. No, I reconsider. I can't keep letting Bianca get to me! The ghost girl didn't hurt me either, so maybe she was harmless. Maybe I could stay. The strange ghost girl *could* still hurt me...or do whatever she wants really though, I think. I should definitely get out of here. Is it too risky to try to leave in the daylight though? I'll never know if I never...*AAACHOO*! I jump back right on time.

"Oh um, sorry about that. I have–ACHOO–allergies," a boy says. I recognize him from the Otter cabin; he is about my height, but a bit wider, with stringy auburn hair. Uhh the one thing I don't need right now is to get sick. Great. Wait, allergies aren't contagious, I think.

"Oh, feel better. I'm going into the woods so..." I say, getting interrupted by ANOTHER SNEEZE! "Do you wanna come with me?" I don't know why I said that. Oh no, what did I do?! Why would I invite anyone to hang out?

He pulls out a tissue from his pocket and wipes his pink nose. "I can be like your assistant. ACHOO!"

"I dunno...you're not going to be my assistant, but you can tag along," I reply, walking up to the edge of the woods. "But no sneezing on me."

"Got it!" he says.

"Oh and what's your name?" I ask.

"Henry," he replies.

"Then let's go, Henry!" I say, pushing my way through a bush. He runs up behind me and shuffles his way through the sage-green leaves.

We walk through the woods for about twenty minutes. There's a small dirt path leading the way through the weeds and grass. Some voices in the distance catch me off guard. "Do you hear that?" I whisper.

"No...why?" he says back in a whisper.

"It sounds like talking. But the thing is...I'm trying to escape from camp, and if we're caught by other kids or adults, then my escape won't work!" I say, heated but still whispering. Oh great, that slipped out! Why in the world did I tell him my plan?!

"Oh. I get it now. The only reason you let me come with you is for backup if you get caught sneaking out. Well in that case, I'm not getting suspended. I'm leaving," he says. But then Henry lets loose the loudest sneeze yet–ACHOO!–just as he turns to go back to camp.

"What was that?!" someone shouts up ahead. I glare at Henry right in the eyes, but he just shrugs.

"Allergies. What can ya do?" he says, then walks right back down the hiking trail through the high trees. I knew that trusting Henry was a bad idea. Oh geez, now I'm definitely going to get caught by whoever is over there. Great. I'm gonna be grounded and *still* stuck at this camp. If I can just sneak around this gate, then I...

"Ahhhhhhhhhhh!" A girl appears in front of me at the gate and screams, then turns to her camera and says, "Now everyone, I might have a Celia exclusive right here in front of you. We just have to ask this girl her name!"

"First of all, you know my name; we're in the Cardinal Cabin! Now, don't ask me questions, and I won't ask you questions," I reply, then start to run ahead. I've learned my lesson about trusting people. You just never know who to trust. That's exactly why I'm alone with no friends. I like it that way.

My foot slips on a patch of sticky mud right before the gate. I slip backward on the wet mud, but someone's tan arms catch me before I fall.

"You alright?" a boy asks, the one who caught me before I fell into the mud puddle.

"Um yeah," I say, quickly getting away from his reach.

"Sorry about Celia. She just wants popularity," he says.

"It's fine." I try to avoid his gaze, but it's impossible, so I change the subject and cut right to the point. "I have to get over this fence."

"Yeah, we've tried. It's really slippery though because our shoes get all wet from the grass," he says. "We turned off the electric shock part at least."

I think for a minute, then realize that we don't need to wear our shoes! "If we go barefoot, then we can obviously just grip on," I say, sliding off my worn, black Nike tennis shoes. I toss them under a tree for now.

"My question is, why do you want to get to the other side? I mean cross the gate," he asks.

I hesitate, but he has genuine eyes and a kind smile that make me tell him the truth. "I wanna escape. From camp. I'm trying to catch a bus or something and hitch a ride home." Ughh why did I tell him *that?!* Oh right, those big, emotional eyes he has.

"Oh, I'm sorry, but the closest bus stop is a few miles from here. You'd have to walk through the woods to not be seen by the counselors," he explains. "And by the way, I'm Lucas. We haven't met properly."

"I'm Hannah. Nice to meet you." I pause, realizing I already know his name; his cabin full of boys sometimes come to ours for parties and stuff. Not that I've ever interacted with any of them. Contemplating, I stare at the wall in front of us. "Ok...I have an idea, but first you have to tell me why *you* want to get to the other side," I say. Before he answers, I attempt to climb the fence. My feet catch the metal edges, but I lose balance and hit the ground, splashing us both with mud.

Lucas wipes his now wet, dirt-covered arms on his shorts, not making fun of me for falling or getting upset. "I want to find the lost treasure," he says. His smile is wide and perfect as he blushes cutely.

But I can't help bursting out laughing. What is he talking about? "Very funny, mister pirate," I say, still laughing.

Lucas looks at his feet and proclaims, "It's true! There *is* a real treasure."

"Ok no. The deal is off then," I say, picturing Lucas in a pirate costume.

"What deal?" Lucas asks dryly.

"I thought you'd never ask. If I help you find whatever you want on the other side, maybe you could drive *me* to the closest bus stop," I say in a whisper so the other few kids gathering around the fence won't hear.

"So how would I *drive* you to a bus stop?" he asks, looking the fence up and down.

"I thought maybe you had your license? Maybe you drove yourself to camp?" I ask, trying not to meet the annoyingly adorable look on his face.

"You thought correct! But first, we need to find the lost treasure. It has gold, diamonds, rubies, jewels, everything!" he says enthusiastically.

"That could pay my aunt's rent for more than either of our lifetimes!" I say, but then quickly realize we have absolutely no idea where this treasure is and how Lucas even knows about it!

I ask him both questions and he replies, "Somewhere on Camp Honey Bear's land lies the treasure of greatness." To the second question, he adds, "I watch many old treasure finding movies and documentaries. People traveled here from across the world to find the hidden treasure. They tried for years to discover this mystery. Eventually, they just gave up searching. No one has succeeded, until us soon!" he finishes dramatically.

"One last question. Who buried this treasure?" I ask, raising my eyebrows at this odd but intriguing boy.

CHAPTER 9

QUESTIONS

Lucas

Hannah is going to help me find the treasure! Finally, I might have a chance to find the thing that made kids at school think I'm too shy to talk. Treasure. I mean, I could become a millionaire with the gold that lies beneath our very feet!

"Lucas! Are you coming?" Celia asks, looking absolutely disgusted by taking off her shoes and going barefoot. She keeps muttering something about "doing it for her social media life."

I might as well take my shoes off too so then I can get up this fence. I chuck my shoes over the fence and start to grip on the wire. I reach the top of the fence and look down. "Ummm guys. How are we supposed to get down from here?" I ask timidly, backing down the fence. Hannah throws her long legs over the fence and then jumps. She hits the ground with a little splat. "Please don't make me do that!" I shout to her from the very top of the fence. Hannah landed so gracefully onto the ground.

She yanks off her sweatshirt and ties it on her waist. "If you don't want your treasure, then..." she says, her voice trailing as she looks up at me. I look down one more time at the grassy ground. *It's not that far, is it?*

"I don't know how to respond to that," I reply, grabbing my leg and slowly lifting it over the fence.

"C'mon, you can do it!" Celia says "Three, two, one…GO!" I imagine that I'll land in a pile of gold as I jump. Nononononono! Ouch! I feel the air for point two seconds, then fall directly into the mud, face first. My eyes are covered in grass and dirt. I regret this. "How do you make it look so easy?" I ask Hannah, mumbling through a mouthful of dirt.

"I don't know…practice in parkour maybe?" she says sarcastically. I bet she has a soft side. I just have to find it.

"Hey guys, do you think you could open the gate door from that side?" Audrey asks, and the others nod in agreement.

"Maybe if I can just *pull* this way," Hannah suggests, picking the lock with a twisted key from her pocket. "It's a moldable key, so I can shape it into any form I'd like." She says this like it's no big deal, though I'm envious she has such an interesting item.

The door whips open with a bang when she opens it. Kim, Oliver, Henry/Sneezy Kid, Audrey, and Celia all come through the door. Celia looks angry because she had to take off her shoes, her brows furrowed.

As we're walking through the forest, Hannah keeps asking me questions about the treasure like: *Who buried it? What are we supposed to do when we find it? How will we know where it is?* "I actually have answers to all of those! First, of course pirates buried it. I think. Second, we'll need to find the map pieces, so once we have them all, we can find the exact location. Third, we can use our hands to dig the treasure up," I reply matter of factly.

"Fine. But I'm not using my hands to dig. That's why shovels were invented," she says. Audrey and Celia nod. Oh and Oliver.

"Where are the map pieces supposed to be?" Henry asks.

"I have the first piece right here!" I reply, pulling out a folded piece of paper with trees and all different markings of Camp Honey Bear's property. It's tinted with green and brown stains.

"Wow!" Henry exclaims, his eyes big as golf balls.

I unfold the paper fully to reveal a map section. "About a year ago, I was traveling with my family. We stopped at a souvenir shop not too far from Camp Honey Bear," I explain. "The old man at the counter said I could have the map piece because he didn't need it anymore." I smooth my hand over the map, like it's a treasure already. "I asked him how *he* managed to find it, and he said his grandmother found it in a bottle, and he's been trying to find the treasure for years after he got the piece of the map. Eventually, he got older and stopped looking."

I watch the others' faces; they have shocked and interested expressions. Most of them are hanging on my every word. "A few weeks after he gave it to me, I did my research and found out where the treasure was last seen. According to the Internet, pirates were all over the seas back in the 1600's, so they needed a place far away from the ocean to bury it. Minnesota was perfect!" I throw my arms out, gesturing at the flourishing woods, the state of rich wilderness and over ten thousand pristine lakes of this state. Birds and squirrels skitter nearby, and I see Celia smack a mosquito on her arm. "The ship's treasure landed exactly on Camp Honey Bear's land. Of course, it wasn't Camp Honey Bear at the time, but still! Hundreds of years later, the camp was built, and no one other than the old man knew about it."

I pause, but everyone is still listening, watching my excited face as I tell the story. "The old man even tried getting a job at the camp to get closer to the treasure. He tried all he could but never succeeded. Basically, the treasure is the main reason I came to this camp!" I finish, a little out of breath. The others look bewildered now. "Maybe that was a little much, but at least I answered all of your questions," I say to Hannah, who still looks blown away.

After that, we walk for a while in silence. The canopy of leaves and needles, skinny to wide tree trunks, bushes of berries and weeds, and animals like chirping birds and rabbits surround us. Apparently, everyone is trying to process what I said while we hike.

I look down at the map and stop in my tracks. "The tree. I think that's where the pirates put the first piece!" I exclaim, astonished that I missed the clue. There is a big marking on the trunk of a tree on the map that's smudged with ink and dirt, but the clue remains noticeable.

"Are you sure it's a tree?" Kim asks. I hold the piece of paper up to her face, and she nods.

We keep walking. Surely we won't miss the huge tree that's hiding our map piece. How obvious will this tree be compared to the others in the woods though? I wonder.

"So when will we find this treasure map piece, and how are we gonna find our way back?! You'll only find out on #Celia'sLifechannel. Keep watching because this is going to be so thrilling as we trudge through these *creepy woods!*" Celia says dramatically, clawing at the air with her hand for drama. CRUNCH! Celia stops her camera and looks down. I turn around.

"Whaaat was that?" Kim asks. Her voice wobbles.

"I'm not sure," Hannah replies.

Audrey rummages through her bag and pulls out a bow and arrow. "Does that work to kill...um you know dangerous animals?" Oliver asks, his voice shaky.

"Yes." Audrey whispers something about not scaring off the prey. CRUNCH! Oliver squeals and grabs onto Kim. She immediately shakes him off, looking annoyed.

"Maybe it was a wolf," Audrey says, confidently pulling back her arrow with her pointer and middle finger.

I have a feeling whatever we heard is close. Too close, I think.

We walk through a patch of berries cautiously. Henry picks one of the berries and throws it up in the air to catch it in his mouth. Oliver slaps the ripe berry before it can land on Henry's tongue, causing it to splat onto the ground. "Poisonous!" Oliver says in the kind of tone your mom would use when you're in trouble.

"You just saved my life," Henry whispers to Oliver. He stares at the berry while we hear another CRUNCH.

Chapter 10

Danger Ahead

Audrey

I laugh dryly at Henry's expression. Then I hear it again! CRUNCH! I whip around, bow and arrow at the ready. I stare through the bushes, spaces between trees and leaves, up at birds chirping from a hole in a tree. Birds are too small to make that noise, I think.

I see rustling from bushes, hear twigs snapping. Some of us gasp. I pull my bowstring taut, arrow poised and ready to shoot. For some weird reason, Hannah shakes her head at me. Oh. I know the reason. Standing about 25 feet away from us is a black bear! A bear who is eating the wild raspberries from the bushes. A bear with razor sharp teeth, midnight black fur, and big, round eyes.

For a minute, my mind just closes. I can't think! I don't know what to do. I just stand there frozen, looking at the bear. Then it hits me! Bow and arrows can kill animals like bears!

I pull back my arrow. But before I can let it soar through the air, the bear stands up from its sitting position, calmly turns around, and walks off into the distance.

I drop my bow and arrow, completely astonished. That was the most terrifyingly quick time of my life! It all went by in less than a minute. Which of course felt like hours.

"That was scary," Kim whispers, shaking and pale.

Oliver looks like he just puked, and Celia is crying a little bit. I walk over to them, and we all start talking about what could've happened. "I didn't even get it on video," Celia mutters, then repeats it in a scream so loud that birds fly from the trees.

"Black bears aren't that aggressive, luckily," Hannah says. "I've read about them before, and screaming is one way to scare him further away," she adds, eyeing Celia.

Slowly, the color comes back to Kim's face. Oliver becomes Oliver again, and Lucas can talk without stumbling over his words. We continue walking north, more aware than before for animals. My footsteps are quieter so we can hear anything else that's life-threateningly dangerous. Lucas halts to a stop.

"Here we are!" he says, grinning at his map piece.

"Where should we look?" Oliver asks.

"For a door next to this tree," Lucas says, walking over to a very old-looking tree with a wide trunk.

"What kind of door are we looking for? Like a door in the ground or a big door or double doors or a fake door or a glass door or..." Hannah's voice trails off, and Lucas looks down at the map and then replies we're looking for a trap door in the ground.

"Okkaaay, " Hannah says slowly.

Everyone digs in the grass, trying to find the "*trap door.*" We continue looking for twenty minutes. Now thirty. Now thirty five. Seems like we've moved every rock, tree branch, fern, or other plant we can, and we've even tried overturning a fallen log.

"Ok, I give up!" I say, falling to the grass. "Usually, I'm not a quitter, but I just don't think it's here!" I say, looking up at the trees' branches and swaying leaves above.

"Maybe it's not here," Oliver says. He sits up against the tree that's supposed to lead to the treasure. "Ouch!" he mumbles.

"What, did you get a splinter from the wood?" Lucas asks, laughing.

"No! As a matter of fact, I didn't," Oliver says. "My arm hit this wood button!" he says, rubbing his elbow, clearly unaware that he just found something great.

I hear a rumbling sound coming from where Hannah's sitting. "That's not just a button! It's our one-way ticket to the trap door!" Hannah says. She stares at something with awe.

"Humph. I'm the true hero now!" Oliver says proudly. He walks over to our growing circle around the opening in the ground.

"Oh please, it was just another accident of yours!" Lucas says. I can tell Lucas is a little jealous that he didn't find it himself.

"I think he did great!" Hannah says, high-fiving Oliver.

I walk over, and my mouth falls open. The wooden door in the ground opened to a staircase! We rush over to the newly-opened door to notice a piece of paper mystically drifting upwards out of the opening! I have no words. My eyes grow very wide as this map piece floats in the air for almost a minute while we all just stare in complete shock.

Then, the silence breaks when Lucas reaches out to touch it, and the paper slowly falls into his hands.

"How did–," I start to ask, but Henry interrupts me.

"Some things are left unexplained," Henry says. I nod slightly.

We snap out of our silent trance, and Kim says, "The button must have led to a chain reaction in the door!" She leans over and studies the mechanics of it. "Yup, just as I thought." I see the wooden geared system underneath.

"But the map," Oliver says, "has no mechanics." The map piece floated on its own, I think.

Oliver digs in his pouch for a while, then pulls out a mini flashlight. He shines it through the tunnel. "It seems as if the staircase is very old. I don't think this is safe."

Despite his protests, Lucas and most of the others charge ahead. "I'll check what type of stone it is!" Oliver says, and he starts to knock on the top step. "Yup, those stairs are definitely not hollow. Still cracked and not safe!"

"Come on, Oliver!" I say, already halfway down the stairs with the others.

"Oh alright," Oliver mumbles to himself. I can already see the tunnel that leads out of the stairwell.

"There's a light up ahead!" Henry yells to us from the bottom of the stairs. The rest of us reach the end of the stairs to find a long, dark and eerie tunnel.

"What do you think is at the end of the tunnel?" I ask Hannah as we start to walk down the dimly lit hall. Flames suddenly light our path from torches on either side of the walls! I jump back from the fire at once, along with everyone else in front of me. How did the fires start on their own? I wonder.

"I bet it'll open back up somewhere else. Or the treasure will be down here," Hannah says, still staring at the magically-lit torches. I shrug and then run back up to the group. Hannah follows.

Lucas grabs one of the torches from the wall and says, "Just in case another animal crosses our path."

I remind him that I have a *perfectly good* weapon in my bag. We start to argue about which weapon is more powerful–my bow and arrows or a fire torch–when the others stare at the flames.

Suddenly, we come to a stop. Kim looks puzzled when she says, "There's a fork in our road.

CHAPTER 11

THE DECISION

Oliver

"So...which way?" I ask, looking straight ahead at the very long tunnel that connects to this one. Then I look at the separate tunnel leading to the right. There's also a third option up into the opening in the stone ceiling that leads back to trees, bushes, and grass. That explains the light from earlier: sunlight.

"I think we only have one choice because this opening doesn't have a ladder to climb up. That makes it almost impossible to get up," Audrey says. "Also, then we would also have to end this expedition. Soooo…"

"Yeah, we're gonna keep going," Henry declares.

"I think I hear something up ahead!" Kim exclaims.

"It's decided then; we keep going straight through the tunnel," Lucas replies.

"What if there are traps up ahead? I mean what if *that's* what Kim heard?" Henry says, fear in his eyes.

"Henry's right. What if there *is* something out there waiting for its prey?" Hannah says.

"And what if that prey is *us*?" I mutter to myself.

"What?" Kim asks me.

"Nothing," I say as we start to walk through the longer tunnel.

"Luckily, *I* brought this bright torch," Lucas says to Audrey, and she glares at him.

In the damp tunnel, there are many carvings on the wall that I stop to look at once in a while, but Henry drags me away from them. Some carvings have twisted snakes or injured people or even people with swords trying to defend themselves from the snakes. Below all of the carvings, there are strange, swirling symbols that make words. They're written in Ancient Egyptian! I took an online class on how to translate these. The wall markings read:

Beware of the snake in a cave underground,

Kill the snake where only one sword can be found

I get nervous after examining the carvings. We can finally see the end of the passageway. I notice the floor has carvings too! Each picture is inside of a small, stone square.

"I knew it! Now we're gonna be burning daylight as we trudge back through an endless tunnel!" Henry says, more frustrated than I've ever seen him.

"Wait!" I say, realizing maybe these carvings mean something. "Carvings! Marks on the floor that are basically a secret code!" I bend down to look at them, but before I can decode the carving, my foot starts to sink into one of the stones.

Huh? As soon as my foot hits the wrong stone, it starts to sink like a trap! Each one of the loose stones that were stepped on fall through the floor. And so do we. I shriek as I fall through the ground, into the unknown. I flail in the darkness as gravity takes me.

I wildly flop around in midair for what feels like a whole minute. Finally, I hit the ground with a thud. I feel a cold, damp, stone floor beneath me. Ouch! My face feels squished against glass. Broken glass. Nooo! My glasses! I reach my hand to my face and feel around. Yeah, definitely broken. I sit up to look down at my shattered glasses, their thin, brown frames cracked.

"Is everyone ok?" Lucas's voice asks next to me.

I hear faint "yeses" from around me. It's very dark here, and to make matters worse, I can't see a thing without my glasses. Two blurry blobs walk over to Lucas. It's wearily quiet here.

Sssssssssssssssssssss! comes a noise, and I shriek.

"Snake!" Kim yells in the distance.

A hand grabs mine and leads me quickly to a safe ledge of stone, where the enemy snakes can't harm me. More blobs come and sit by me on the ledge. I feel like I can barely breathe, I'm so panicked.

"Throw me the torch!" Audrey shouts to Lucas. They are both still on the snake-infested ground.

"The flames burnt out when we fell!" Lucas replies in a yell.

I manage to put my shattered glasses on–and see a snake coiling around Audrey's waist below the ledge! An urge to do something I've never done before or never even thought of doing hits me like a punch in the stomach. I have to save her!

Far off, through a small body of water and across the shore on the other side of the dark cave, I see a tiny golden shape. My heart hammers in my chest as I prepare to jump down from the ledge.

The golden object is shiny and hanging on the stone wall behind a swampy pool of water. It's a sword! The same sword I saw in the carvings! It said, *beware of the snake in a cave underground, kill the snake where only a sword can be found.* It can kill the snake!

I jump down from the stone ledge and hit the slick, wet ground. I run faster than ever. I charge through what feels like slime from the snake beneath my feet. Then it's wet. Very wet and cold. Both things I hate. I run through the dark pool. The water soaks me up to my waist now.

Seconds later, a rushing wave knocks me under the water. Another cold tide washes over me. How are waves coming in? I run through the water to notice the drop off. I'm now swimming through the water with the courage of a shark.

A blurry blob far behind me starts yelling. Saying something about water and multiple snakes. I'm surprised I haven't reached the other side yet. Another wave pushes me forward with the strongest surge of all.

Finally, I reach the muddy shore. I stand up, covered in mud and soaked from head to toe. Then a thought occurs to me: what if the snake already suffocated Audrey?

I start yelling and calling for the snake; hopefully it'll release her and come for me. It's hard enough to see without my glasses. Why does it have to be so dark? Hopefully, the snake released her and is coming for me. *Oh gosh, now I'm hoping for a giant beast of a snake to come for me? Who am I turning into?*

I look across the navy-blue lake. A big, long shadow is sliding away from Audrey and slinking to cross the lake. I wonder how the others are doing? Maybe there are other snakes like this one? I push the thought aside and reach for the golden sword.

As I pull the sword out of the stone wall, it loosens, but when I yank it out, the rocky wall starts to rearrange into a big, dark hole where the sword once was. The sword clanks as it falls to the ground.

A slimy, cold object coils around my neck from the hole. I hyperventilate as I start grabbing at the snake. It only grips tighter! I manage to get my hand through and I grab the sword from the ground. A gush of water sucks me in toward the newly-revealed hole.

The shiny, golden sword is heavier than I thought, but I can lift it. I bring the sword up and stab the snake so hard, I feel a little bit of the sword's tip scraping at my skin. The snake falls to the ground, along with the golden sword that saved me. I shiver and ring my shirt out, which is now also dripping with snake blood.

"Oliver! Come back!" Kim yells, still standing on the stone ledge with Henry.

But before I can respond to them, I get sucked backward by a frigid, vicious wave. I struggle to breathe, inhaling bitter, tangy, and rotten-tasting water. I flail my arms and legs in the cool blueness, and my head goes under. The water doesn't relent, propelling me deeper while I struggle to swim. Then it all goes black…

Chapter 12

Escape

Kim

"That was insane!" Lucas yells to Oliver, who just saved Audrey's life! He looks around for Oliver in the darkness.

"Where is he?" I ask, worried that we won't be able to find him.

"He disappeared after that loud rushing noise," Audrey says. We call Oliver's name for a long time and search in the pond, across the lake, and everywhere in the dark room. Tiny garter snakes slither harmlessly in the water, but the giant one is dead, thanks to Oliver.

"We have to keep looking," I say, drenched from the lake. I feel bad about leaving someone behind. He couldn't have gotten far.

"We can't just leave him for dead. Oliver could swim, right?" Hannah asks, eyebrows raised. She looks so concerned.

"I don't know what could've happened to him! The noise started when Oliver pulled the sword from the stone wall," Lucas says, peering at the wall. "But Kim is right. We have to keep looking!" he says, stepping out of the pond. I nod, thinking he can't be dead, *right?*

"I kind of wish you would disappear," Audrey mutters to Lucas. He glares at her.

Henry groans and says, "Can you both stop fighting?! We're all stuck down here in this pit! The only way out is up, ok? We have to keep going." Everybody nods at his outburst, since he makes sense.

"Yes, but let's keep looking for Oliver along the way. Keep calling his name," Hannah adds. We all agree, hoping and praying we find him soon. We head back to the long tunnel, past the pool, and find a huge rock wall above with a ledge.

Hannah looks around the room, saying, "I watched the show *American Ninja Warriors* every Saturday with my aunt when I was little."

"I wonder how that's gonna help us?" Henry says sarcastically.

"One of the obstacles kind of looks like this giant indent in the wall leading up to a ledge! It's called the warp wall. It's like a big curved wall that you run up; maybe we could try to run up to the top!" Hannah takes five huge steps backward, then gains momentum and runs up the big rock, feet moving quickly, arms pulling her over the ledge at the brink. "Accomplished!" she yells down at us.

I walk over to the wall and try to slowly climb to the top by finding a little indent to put my hand in.

"That's not how you do it! You have to run up like I did," Hannah says.

"Okay, I'll try it," I grumble, since I'm not a huge fan of heights. Still, I back up and sprint. I start to run up the rock, but slip backwards and hit the ground with a thud. My ankle twists to the side, and I wince.

"Are you ok?" Celia asks.

"I think I twisted my ankle," I say as the pain shoots through my foot. Celia hovers over me, acting like a doctor. She touches a part of my foot and I reply that *yes, that hurts!* The others are starting to run up the wall/rock. "I don't think I'll be able to get up the warp wall." I gaze at the others on the top of the wall.

"Maybe we can tie one of these vines around your waist, and all of us at the top of the wall can pull you up," Henry yells down at me and Celia. He points to a length of thick, evergreen vines growing out of the rock up there.

"I guess, but how will we know if the ropes are sturdy enough?" Celia asks Henry, crossing her arms.

"Like this!" he yells, and it echoes across the wide cave. He launches the vine over a root in the ceiling. He lunges forward, still gripping the vine as he swings through the air and lands on yet another tall ledge of stone across the room. "I think it will hold!" Henry shouts from the other side of the cave.

We all laugh, and one by one they start to swing on the vine while I wait down on the ground. Celia, Hannah, and Audrey stay behind to help tug me up the wall. I watch Hannah swing across to the ledge, looking like an acrobat. Celia offers to go with me on the vine swing, but I say, "It probably can't hold both of us at the same time."

"Ok. You can go first then," she offers.

I grab onto the vine, take a few steps backwards (very gingerly on my injured ankle) and then jump off of the tall ledge. My hair blows back as I fly through the air. Hannah helps me down to the ledge because my feet don't quite reach it.

"Hey guys! This kind of looks like the wooden button that Oliver found, but in lever form." Henry points to a lever on a concave portion of the wall.

"Pull it already!" Celia says, taking out her camera. Her face falls to a frown when she sees the cracked screen. Poor Celia, I think. She obviously loved that thing, and a fancy camera like that isn't cheap.

Henry pulls the lever, and the wall suddenly rearranges into three holes. The lowest of the holes has water being sucked into it from the lake. The highest of the holes has water hurdling out of it, and the middle hole is completely still with nothing coming in or out. It's like natural waterworks.

"I think Oliver was sucked into a hole," I say with a jolt of realization. "If he was sucked backward, then we need to go into the lowest hole. It's the only possibility." I look down at the hole closest to the ground.

"Ok, but what if that hole is the most dangerous? Just because Oliver was sucked into it doesn't mean it's gonna be safe," Lucas says.

"It doesn't matter. The most important thing is to find Oliver!" Celia interrupts.

"Yeah Lucas, someone's life is more important than treasure!" Audrey says. She points to the three options in the stone.

"Besides, don't you know the saying *first is the worst, second is the best, third is the one with the treasure chest?*" Hannah adds, laughing.

"Haha, very funny. That's totally gonna make me want to go," Lucas says sarcastically. Everyone glares at him. "Fine, I'll vote for the third hole with the treasure chest," Lucas says, jumping down from the ledge and into the swampy water. "Yippee!" Lucas's yells echo throughout the cave as he streams through the water.

"Umm, you're sure he's gonna be alright?" Celia asks. She glances at my swollen ankle.

"Almost positive," I say, biting my lip. "I'll go next." I prepare to plunge into the cold water. "We should go in pairs to make sure no one gets hurt." I hope they don't hear the worry in my voice.

Henry says, "Celia and I will go together and Hannah, Kim, and Audrey will go together."

Hannah smiles at me. Then Celia grips his hand, and with this kind act, we jump into the lake. The water tunnel looks almost like the start of a water slide, just dirtier and older. We're sucked into the hole, like water down a drain or bathtub.

Celia screams something from inside the slide, and Henry screams something back. I glide and shout, giddy with the speed before I crash into the water. The cold lake water feels refreshing on my hurt ankle, too.

"Let's find this treasure!" I yell.

CHAPTER 13

THE FOURTH STEP

Lucas

I'm the first to enter the tunnel, and it's a long ride down. The water pulls me down the tunnel like a slide. I see the opening at the bottom about 40 seconds after, and I fly out into much warmer water than the slimy pool. I push off of the sharp ground underwater.

As soon as my head is out of the water, I see a beautiful waterfall in front of me. The whole cavern sparkles with glittering, purple and blue crystals. There are underwater crystals! That explains why the ground was sharp. My first thought is that I'm rich already, but I realize crystals aren't worth a lot anyway. They're not diamonds, I think.

Something moves in the distance, rippling in the water. Assuming it's another snake, I dive under the water again. After about a minute, I can't hold my breath any longer, so I come up for a little breath of air, but instead of a snake…I see Oliver! He's standing right across from the little stream I'm treading in.

Splash! I turn around to see Celia and Henry. "Oliver! Kim was right! She picked the right tunnel!" Henry says after emerging out of the water.

"I wonder what the other tunnels lead to," Celia says with a frightened look.

"Well, we don't need to find out!" Hannah yells, plunging into the stream, followed by Audrey and Kim.

"It looks like I chose the right tunnel," Kim says, climbing out of the water to hug Oliver. We all follow and pile out of the clear, sparkling water that reflects the pristine crystals.

"I knew you'd find me!" Oliver says, accepting his hug. When we part, we explore the cave, which glows with the bright crystals like frosted mirrors.

Though it's beautiful, we trudge around the cave for over two hours. "The whole cavern is just one big maze!" Oliver explains.

"Yeah, I think we found that out," Celia says, glancing down at her phone and camera, which were both broken by her fall. She can't take any pictures or videos now sadly.

"At least we'll have plenty of crystals when we leave," Hannah says. She breaks off a few stunning pieces of the crystals and puts them in her pocket.

"If we can even find our way back to camp. When we went through the tunnel, we didn't really have a plan to get back up," Kim says wearily. She glances around and limps slightly due to her ankle.

"Marco!" Henry yells.

"Polo," we all say back to him for the fifth time.

About twenty minutes later, we're all groaning because of the hunger that's been dragging us since Henry almost ate a poison berry.

"Anyone want a soggy orange?" Oliver asks, pulling it out of his pouch, which he duct-taped to his pants. We all start yelling at him because he's had food the whole time.

"Fine, I guess I'll eat it," Oliver says, peeling the bottom. We all lunge for Oliver, but he jumps backwards. "Maybe we can share then, geez."

"Seven people. One orange. I don't think so," Audrey says angrily.

"Dude, give me the orange," Henry says, grabbing at it like an upset toddler.

"Guys, guys. Calm down; I bet he has more fruit or other food in his pouch," I say, looking at Oliver with hopeful eyes.

"Well actually..." Oliver says, digging through his little pouch, "I ate the rest when I came down here. I didn't think you guys would even realize I was missing, so I started stress eating my sandwich, carrots, chips, fruit snacks, and granola."

"YOU WHAT?" Audrey yells. She snatches the orange.

"Let's cut the orange into six parts with a sharp crystal, so we can all have some," I suggest.

"But I'm the seventh person," Oliver says.

We all shoot him a look, and I say, "Sorry man. You already had your dinner." Then, we slowly eat our slice of orange, savoring every bite.

"We need to find a way out!" I say, then suck the last of the juice out of my orange slice.

"I wanna go home and play Fortnight," Henry says.

"Yes! I haven't posted anything on Instagram, Tik Tok, YouTube, or Twitter for almost a whole day!" Celia exclaims.

"We can't give up yet! We already have two pieces of the map. Plus, we already found a secret staircase, a tunnel of doom with cobras, and a crystal cavern!" I say thinking about everything we've encountered so far.

"Bro, you sound like Dora the Explorer," Henry says. And we all laugh hysterically for the first time in the last three hours.

CHAPTER 14

A WAY OUT

Henry

"Ok, so water led us down here, so I bet water can lead us back up," Celia says, gazing at the stream for answers.

"Maybe," Lucas says. "It's a good theory at least."

"I think the waterfall has something to do with it. I mean, why would a waterfall be down this *deep* underground?" I ask.

Hannah walks over to us and sticks her hand right into the pouring waterfall. "There's definitely a space back there."

"I'm not getting wet *again*. I'm just starting to dry off!" Celia whines.

Hannah is already walking straight through it, the waterfall's cascade streaming over her. "Yup! There's an entire room back here, but it's really dark."

"Use my mini flashlight!" Oliver yells, chucking it into the waterfall. It splays through, making a small space that the water closes around like a mouth.

"Thanks."

"I always have a spare."

We all wait in the waterfall's mist as it roars. "So?!" Audrey asks a few seconds later.

"It's a whole river with even more crystals than before!" Hannah explains. "And there's four wooden boats that we can use!"

Audrey walks up to the waterfall and steps through it like a mystical water spirit. "Wow," Audrey says quietly but still loud enough for us to hear her over the rushing waterfall.

"Uhh whatever," Celia says, flinching when she walks through the waterfall. Everyone else follows her. I'm last to walk through. The water's warmer than I expected and less powerful.

When I enter the new area, the whole place glitters brightly. I take a few steps up to the rainbow water. I realize it's all rainbow-colored because the crystals growing on the ceiling reflect into the river. Just then, every crystal in sight lights up with a fluorescent glow, making the whole cavern sparkle. My eyes grow wide as we all stare at the magic-like scene.

"We can take the boats down the stream," Lucas says, sort of snapping out of our daze at the glowing walls and ceiling. We all get in the boats, which are old-fashioned wood with robust oars to row them. Lucas is with Hannah, Audrey's with Celia, and Oliver is with

Kim. That leaves me on the last boat. I took canoeing lessons when I was four, so hopefully I'll be catching up.

We row down the stream for a good five minutes, taking in the beautiful crystals everywhere.

"God, I wish I had my camera," Celia says with awe.

"I know, right? Sorry yours broke," I reply, paddling along next to her boat.

"I think we're the first people to find this place in probably a century or two," Kim says, fiddling with her glasses.

"Yeah, I bet you're right. I mean all of these underground ruins and caves and tunnels and waterfalls! We could be legendary if we end up finding the treasure," I say, and everyone agrees.

"We're here," Lucas says when our boats start to slow. The stream comes to a circular pond at its end and a chocolate-brown dock. Lucas reaches to grab the dock's end.

We tie the boats up to the dock and take one last look at the colorful crystals. Then he turns and says, "Look, there's a door up ahead." I notice a giant, wooden door with a huge key hole in the center. This is the weirdest cave, I think.

"How are we supposed to get through it?!" Oliver asks.

I walk up to the door and pull on the handle, and the whole handle rips off! Like it was older than the treasure map. "You've got to be kidding me!" I shout.

"Now what?" Oliver asks.

"We'll have to live in this cave forever," Audrey groans.

"Maybe if we find the key somewhere," I say.

"I have a moldable key, remember?" Hannah says, pulling out the small, play-dough-like block. With quick fingers, she starts to mold it into a key shape. "Ugggghh it's too big of a keyhole," Hannah says in frustration.

"Like I said, maybe we can *find the key somewhere,* " I tell her.

"Look what I found!" Audrey says excitedly with perfect timing. We all run over to her, and she shows us a small lever under her seat in the wooden boat.

"Pull it!" Kim says. *Crank!* She heaves the lever, a latch on the side of the boat opens, and a huge wood key drops out.

"Yes! Now we can open the door," Lucas says as he grabs the key and races to the door. He turns the key, and our escape route opens with a click.

CHAPTER 15

LOST AND FOUND

Celia

"What's inside?" I ask cautiously.

"A staircase," Lucas replies, then walks through the door and starts to climb the stairs leading up to the light. We follow behind him.

"Wait," I say. I notice fine letters etched into one of the staircase's rock steps. A note. "Can anyone read," I have no idea what language it's written in as I ask, "umm…these weird letters?"

"It's Egyptian," Oliver says confidently. Everyone starts asking why there would be Ancient Egyptian writings in Minnesota, but Oliver says he'll explain later. Oliver translates it like this: *Press the button above the stairs to reveal a piece of the map, but beware.*

We lunge for the small button above the stairs. Apparently no one wants to *beware*. When I tap the circular, stone button, another piece of the map pops out of the wall! And as soon I have a firm grip on the map section, the door down at the bottom of the staircase slams shut.

I gasp, and others let out surprised yelps. The next second, latches on the walls open, appearing out of nowhere, and sand starts spilling out of them.

"Quicksand!" I scream. Out of one of the latches comes a shovel. It falls into the sand below. "Lucas! That shovel is probably for digging up the treasure! Maybe it's a special shovel we need!" I say.

"No way! I'm not letting you get hurt for a stupid treasure," he yells to me over the loud sound of pouring sand, which is like sandpaper rain, grainy and scratchy.

"I have to!" I yell, but I'm not sure why I'm so determined. I shouldn't be risking my life for treasure. Yet I could buy a new camera, new phone, and SO much more after we hit it rich!

"You'll get sucked into the sand!" Hannah shouts, and Lucas yells something in agreement, but it's hard to hear over the loud sand pouring down on us.

"Just pull me out then!" I run down the stairs and jump into the sticky sand. I move my hands around for the shovel until I finally find something hard, solid. When I try to yank the shovel's handle, my hand is stuck in place; it won't budge.

"Lucas, this would be a good time to pull me out! Be my hero!" I scream, starting to sink under. I'm still gripping tightly onto the shovel.

"We've got you!" screams Kim as they all grab my arms and tug me hard. But it's no use now. The sand rubs against my skin, rough like dry concrete. *Who knew pouring sand could be so heavy?* I think, my heart hammering with fear.

Though I scream and squirm, the sand reaches my neck. My friends clutch my hands, hauling with all their might. But my head is swallowed by sand. I try to breathe, but I keep inhaling the sand until my throat feels like it's clogged. My eyes are very blurred and itchy, but I still have a firm grasp on the shovel. I try to open my mouth to scream again, but nothing comes out.

It's been too long. I'm not gonna make it. My eyes flit shut, and I'm engulfed into the blackness of what feels like the end.

What is that though? A touch of something grasping my arms, lifting me. I feel twelve strong hands hoist me out of the misery, then cool air all around me. There's moonlight shining on me, and it's so nice to be out of the sand. I'm relieved, but I can still taste the terrible scratchiness in my throat.

When my friends set me down on the stairs, my vision is still a little blurry, but I can make out the objects around me. I sit up and loudly cough out every last sand grain in my mouth. My whole body still feels like sandpaper, but I stand up anyway and tell everyone I'm fine.

We all scramble up the stairs until we reach the top. We're covered in sticky sand, but I can see through an opening on top of the staircase that it's almost pitch black outside. Thank goodness for the moonlight filtering in.

When we finally reach the top, back aboveground, Oliver pulls out some matches from his pouch. We gather sticks and start a small fire to keep the gnats, mosquitos, and bigger animals away. Setting up camp is harder than it sounds, trying to keep the fire from going out every five minutes and making our beds out of pine needles, leaves, and grass.

I lay down on the uncomfortable bed I've crafted, holding the hopefully special shovel, and start to think, what the heck I was doing basically *flirting* with Lucas?! Asking him to be my hero? Was I trying to impress him by jumping in the sand? We've all learned he has eyes for Hannah, the way they stare at each other and tease back and forth. And not to mention Kim falling head over heels for him, following him around everywhere like a lost puppy. I shake off the guilty feeling and close my eyes, though my empty stomach rumbles.

*****

The next morning, I wake up even hungrier.

"Ok, what's for breakfast?" I ask. "I'm starved; we haven't eaten since yesterday morning. Crazy, but the sixth of an orange I had for dinner doesn't count," I add, glaring at Oliver.

"Guys, guys, maybe there's another berry bush around here. You know, non-poisonous," Henry suggests. We all start to rise, but before we can, a voice hollers in the wood's outskirts.

"Hey! Kids! Come back to camp! We've been looking for you for a whole day! We looked everywhere!" the voice calls.

I turn around to see one of the older camp counselors.

"Umm...what do we do now?" Henry asks.

"I have a plan, sort of," Hannah whispers. We all walk about ten feet further into the forest and huddle.

"We have to distract him somehow, so I can dig the treasure out," Lucas says. I offer him the shovel I nearly died for.

I start to walk away, pondering this so-called plan when I realize we don't have a next step. "What are we supposed to do after that? Grab the treasure and run?" I ask Lucas.

"I don't know," he says.

"I guess that's a plan," I tease him. While I roll my eyes, he just smiles with his perfect teeth. God, why does he have to have cute dimples too?

Everyone except Lucas runs over to the tall counselor man, and we start rambling on about how we've been lost for so long and we need water and food. Meanwhile, Lucas starts to dig in the place it says to on the map piece I found in the staircase wall.

"I'm just glad you're all okay." He smiles. Then, he commands, "Come back to camp with me now!" He turns around and starts walking.

"No! Umm…we need you to go back to camp first and get us something to drink because we're too thirsty to walk," Henry says.

"Yeah right kid; let's go already! You're going to be in so much trouble when I bring you all back." He turns and starts to walk, but shortly after, he realizes nobody is following him. "Come on. What's the hold up?"

"This," Lucas says, pulling a small golden box out of the ground. The man's face fades into a shocked look of pleasure.

"Wow, it's real," the counselor mutters, and I think it's quite odd he would say that because he doesn't know what it is. Or does he?

"That can't be it," I say, "That box is only as big as the palm of my hand."

"Open it!" Henry says eagerly. The strange counselor nods, eyes wide, grinning like crazy.

"Big things come in small packages," Lucas says, reaching for the latch on the box.

CHAPTER 16

ALMOST, BUT NOT QUITE

Audrey

"What have you kids been up to? You've been mischievous behind my back!" the middle-aged counselor says. His voice is shallow and deep with a hint of twang.

"Nothing, nothing. We just…ahh…we…" Oliver tries, but he's terrible at lying.

I hear a rustling noise in the bushes. I gulp, thinking it might be another bear or animal that wants to eat us. I reach for my bow, but can't get to it fast enough. Surprisingly, the noise was coming from an old man! He steps from the bushes and says to the camp counselor, "Oh, these kids are mine, Conner. I'm teaching them the ways of the wild for real back here," the wrinkled man says. How do Ben and Conner know each other's names? Are they friends, enemies, or even related somehow?

"If these seven kids don't get back to their cabins in the next ten seconds, I'm going to have to call their parents and tell them that they'll need to be picked up from camp right away!" the camp counselor Conner says, his face turning a shade of red.

"I'm afraid there won't be any need for that, Conner. I will stay with the kids until they're ready to come back to camp themselves," the old man states calmly.

"I'm a fully grown man, and you do not have to tell me what to do anymore, Ben."

"I'm aware of that. You may go now, Conner," Ben says.

"Fine! You'll be hearing from my boss!" Conner shouts as he storms off through the woods.

"That was awesome!" Henry says to Ben.

"You totally saved us from getting in trouble!" Oliver adds.

"Hey, aren't you the man from the souvenir shop?!" Lucas asks.

"I sure am."

"How do you know that Conner guy anyway?" I ask.

"He's my nephew."

CHAPTER 17

BREAKFAST AT BEN'S

Hannah

"Then why is he so rude to you?" Henry asks Ben.

"I can answer all of your questions over breakfast," Ben replies.

"You brought," Henry starts smiling, "breakfast?"

"Sorry, we haven't eaten for a while," Audrey says.

"No, no that's alright," Ben says. "My small cottage and souvenir shop aren't too far."

"But first, we need to open the box!" Lucas says loudly. After Conner's interruption, we can finally see what's inside. Lucas lifts the little gold latch on the front of the box. And it opens. Inside the little box is the last piece of the map! We lay out all of the four pieces on the ground. Piece by piece, we complete it and figure out where we need to go next.

"By the looks of it, the next place we have to look is…right under Ben's souvenir shop?!" Lucas says, his face shocked. "The whole time the treasure was where it all started!"

Ben shakes his head in surprise. "Really? I've been searching for that treasure for almost 60 years, and all along it's been under my store?! I just can't believe it." He looks amazed, eyebrows raised, and has to sit down on a log to process this information.

Soon, we head toward Ben's cottage. But we hear something in the bushes around 20 feet away. We all remain still, in case it's a bear again. Out comes a mother fox and three little pups. It's adorable!

"Foxes are a sign of good luck," Audrey whispers. The red fox mother walks up to a little stream of water. The fox crosses on a log as the little pups follow, puffy tails wiggling. The mother has a small piece of meat in her mouth. Then the fox family crawls into a little den behind some rocks. It was cool to see those shy creatures in the wild.

We don't say a peep for the rest of the walk to Ben's cottage. "I think we're here," Lucas says. There's a clearing where Ben's tiny house sits.

"My shop is a little farther down by the highway," Ben says, digging through his pockets for a house key. He finds it in one of his many cargo pants pockets. Ben unlocks the door and pushes it open.

We walk inside. He gives us a little tour of the cabin. To the right is a small kitchen area, and to the left is a living room with a big couch and rocking chair, along with a fireplace and a small wooden dining table.

"We might as well eat some breakfast," Ben says, taking the bacon and eggs out of the fridge. We all sit down at the round dining table. Our map shows exactly where Ben's shop is, but of course when the map was made Ben's shop wasn't there. Well, a house-shaped marking is drawn in the exact place, but that's impossible, right?

"So Ben, how long has your shop been there?" Kim asks. She sits across from me.

"Over 100 years! It was built almost a century before. My dad bought it and fixed it up when I was ten," Ben replies. "Breakfast will be done in about 15 minutes, so you kids can keep reading the map, see if we missed anything."

"We've looked at it 1,000 times, but it's hard to tell when they're just pieces," I say, exaggerating.

"I have a roll of scotch tape if you want to tape the map together," Ben says, and he hands me a roll from another pocket of his cargo pants.

For breakfast, we have scrambled eggs, bacon, toast, and orange juice. I'm so full, and the cottage smells like bacon grease. Ben bandages Kim's sprained ankle too.

"Let's get to all of your questions," Ben says after he helps Kim.

"Yeah, why was Conner so mad at you?" Kim asks.

Ben sighs. "Here's the whole story. When I was around 19, I was a counselor at Camp Honey Bear. I had lots of hobbies, like fishing and checkers and fixing things up, but my biggest interest was in pirates. Ever since I was a boy, I've loved the stories my father would tell me." He smiles. "I was fascinated by the gold and treasure and swords."

Ben continues, "One night, we found out my grandmother, Eleanore Rennald, was dying. She only had a little time left to live when she gave me a bottle. Inside it was a scroll. A map. I knew for the rest of my life I needed to find whatever Eleanore was looking for. For her. I was desperate." We nod along as he shakes his head. "My brother died in a car accident 28 years later, and I took in his son, Conner. The second Conner got his hands on that map, he set out to look for the treasure. Every day and night, he spent hours searching. Eventually, summer ended, and I went back to the store and Conner grew up and got a job and forgot about me. I kept looking for the treasure for my grandma, but I never got so focused on it like Conner." Ben folds his arms on the table. "Conner was fired from his last job because he lost his temper over a promotion that wasn't given to him. He became a camp counselor here just like I was. But he got a small salary working here at my shop too." He motions down the road to his store.

"I saw him sneak out every night to try to find the treasure and the other pieces of the map. Of course, he never found it because he didn't have the pieces like you do. He got so angry…every night he would go out into the woods and just yell and scream. Even when he was a kid, I knew something was wrong with him, but he got worse when his dad died. He changed, and not for the better." Ben's eyes turn sad, and he glances out the window at the forest. "I tried to talk to him calmly about the treasure, but he was dead set on finding it. He lost his mind."

We wait while Ben pauses. He blinks a couple of seconds away and goes on."Then Conner took his life savings and bought beer and a fancy new car. He came back a month after, and I warned him he can't survive on those two things. He stuck with the counselor job for a long time after that. Never talked to me again, embarrassed that I was right. Then one day, when Lucas showed up at my shop and asked to look at the map, he had that same expression I had when I first got it. I saw it in his eyes." Lucas blushes and grins at Ben. "So I let him have it. I was too old for treasure hunting, and besides those days were over. Simply letting go of my lifelong mission ended up pretty great now that we're minutes away from finding the gold," Ben finishes.

"We better start looking soon," Henry says. We agree, get our muddy shoes on, and walk out the door.

We start to walk down a path through the woods, Ben leading the way. We walk for about four blocks (well what would be four blocks in a city like I'm used to), and then we see a small shop sitting by the road. It's made of brick with a fading green roof. There's one small window. A worn down metal sign creeks in the wind, and a red cardinal sits on the top of the sign, watching us carefully. I immediately think of Michelle, the Cardinal Cabin counselor.

"We better hurry before someone else finds us," I say and start to walk up the stone steps. Ben unlocks the door and we head inside. There are old trinkets and statues and books everywhere.

"Where did you get all these?" Kim asks Ben.

"Oh here and there. Remember, I've been in business for longer than you all have been alive." We follow Ben to the basement.

"Let me see the map," I say, snatching it from Lucas. I see him smile out of the corner of my eye.

We walk down a flight of creaky stairs in silence. The basement is deserted, except for one big painting hanging on the wall. It's a picture of the stars, the Big Dipper and the Little Dipper. We smooth out the map on the dusty floor. "If we're here, then we'd have to turn north, walk straight forward a few feet and then…" My voice trails off while I keep my eyes on the map's coordinates.

I walk closer to the painting, then keep studying the map. My head doesn't move. I can't look up. Too much at stake. Then I feel a hand gently lift my chin. It's Lucas. The moment is everlasting, his warm hand on my cheek. Butterflies form in my stomach and for a second we're so close I'm almost positive he's going to make a move, but they fly away when I see the tiny blonde ghost girl in a flash. *The girl* who vanished into thin air right in front of me.

I inhale a breath when I realize it's her. She climbs through the window well and just stands there in plain sight. Lucas's eyes follow mine, but I can tell he doesn't see her. No one else notices the ghost girl but me. And out of nowhere a big drop of water splashes on the girl's nose. I blink and she's gone. This has to somehow be my mind playing tricks on me. If she's real, is this ghost linked to the treasure? Why is she appearing here and now? At least she didn't talk this time.

Suddenly my mind goes blank; all that matters in this world is me and Lucas, standing here in the shadow of this starry painting. Slowly, I lean in to do something I never would've dreamed of doing in this moment. *Kiss him,* I tell myself. We're just inches away from each other when the sound of a *gunshot* eats away the silence and stutters my heart.

CHAPTER 18

A HIDDEN PLACE

Lucas

I think I must have screamed at the gunshot, but soon I realize no one screamed. Then why did I hear a girl scream? It came from right behind the painting–but it wasn't me, Hannah, Kim, Celia, Oliver, Henry, or Audrey. Then who was it? Everything goes still.

"Give me the map," a familiar voice says slowly. I turn around to see Conner standing in the doorway of the stairwell. He's wearing a checkered pattern shirt and a bandanna. He holds a gun in his hand. "I figured you had found the whole map by now, Ben," he spits.

I'm still in the shadows with Hannah, my hands around her waist and hers on my neck. We awkwardly back away from each other and I mindlessly slip the map behind the painting. It's hollow behind the canvas. I hear the sound of paper brushing against the inside behind the painting.

"Don't you point that thing at me," Ben says, standing by the low window. He digs around in the window well when another gunshot echoes against the walls of the basement. I flinch and close my eyes.

By instinct, I grab Hannah's hand, and she looks at me; she's pale and shaking. Conner shot through the ceiling.

"All you kids on the ground NOW! Hands on your heads!" Conner shouts. We do what he says. "Who has the map?" he asks in a creepy whisper. None of us respond, now on the cold floor with our hands on our heads. Some tears fall from Celia's eyes on the right of me. Hannah looks scared, and I am too.

Conner paces back and forth. "Talk now, or you'll never get to again," he warns.

I swallow hard, trying not to cry. Conner sighs and shoots through the glass window, missing Ben by an inch. The bullet's sound hurts my ears. "I need my treasure!" Conner screams.

Ben emerges from the window well and points yet another gun at Conner. "Now, let's not get messy here. Just drop the gun and let these kids go. They're innocent."

Conner starts to laugh when…BOOM! Ben shoots Conner's rifle out of his hand, and it drops to the ground with a thud.

Ben walks up to him calmly. "Listen Conner, you were glad I didn't send you to the cops years ago. You won't be glad anymore." He kicks Conner's leg and takes his bandanna from around his neck. He uses the bandanna to tie Conner's hands behind his back and drops him to the floor. Ben picks up the gun in front of his nephew's nose. He drags Conner upstairs and dials 911. Meanwhile, we sit up, catching our breath, trying to process the danger we were just in.

"You kids get up here and take my car. It's old, but it'll do."
We run upstairs as a group, my heart still thundering. "I don't want
the cops asking questions about what we've found or how you
haven't been seen in almost three days now when they get here," Ben
says while he tapes Conner's cursing mouth shut.

Before we go outside with Ben's car keys, I whisper, "I found
a hollow room behind the painting. I slipped the map behind the
painting. It's safe until we come back."

"How will we get to it?" Kim asks.

"We can come back when the police clear out, but we need to
get as far away as possible right now," I explain. We walk past the
squirming man on the ground. Celia raises her middle finger at
Conner as we all rush to the car.

CHAPTER 19

DRIVING

Hannah

We all pile into the old 1990's Volvo. It's really light turquoise blue and looks almost like it was from a movie. I'm in the passenger seat, and Lucas is driving. Kim, Oliver, and Celia are behind us, and, in the way back, Henry and Audrey sit together.

We drive a few miles south, and there's nothing but cornfields for as far as I can see. Trying to shake out our nerves from Conner, we try to have fun and forget that ever happened. So we crank the radio and have a blast. Lucas is singing along, and I try not to make eye contact with him. After we almost kissed, it's kind of awkward. I could tell he's liked me ever since the start of camp, and now I'm sort of falling for him too.

He turns down the radio, and a thought seems to hit him. "Hannah, the deal was if you helped me find the treasure, I would drive you home," he says sadly.

"Um I...I've changed my mind. I thought camp was all crafts and canoeing, but it's way more. I've made more friends here than I've made in my whole life. We're kind of a family now. A camp family," I say. Everyone cheers, and I open the dashboard compartment to find a full lemonade can.

"To us!" I say, popping the can's metal tab so we can all taste it. We pass around the lemonade, enjoying the citrusy tang. Then we roll down the windows, feel the wind in our hair, and just act like regular kids…not rebels running away from camp, trying to find a hidden treasure.

We all talk and drink lemonade for about 10 minutes and confess things we've done in the past. Nothing any of us has done compares to what we've accomplished in the past two days. It feels like we've known each other for years and not days.

I think of all of the sand and dirt and gunk I've swam through and look down to see how gross I must be though. My own blood also stains my shirt a little. It's probably nothing, but I lift up my shirt to check. Touching the blood with my index finger, a splintering pain seeps through me. Everyone's still cheering and yelling and overall acting silly.

"Guys!" I raise my voice to make them stop screaming. "I've been shot.

CHAPTER 20

WORRY

Celia

"That psycho shot you?!" I say, scared and angry but digging my nails into my romper to make the emotions go away. But they don't go away.

"Conner's shot may have ricocheted in the basement and hit her," Audrey says in a gasp.

"We need to call a doctor," Lucas says, turning pale with shock.

"There isn't anything for 50 miles," Oliver says as he looks at his GPS he pulled from his pouch.

Hannah breathes heavily and starts to panic. She opens the door while the car is still moving. Lucas abruptly stops the car and looks at Hannah with a panicked face. "I have to get out of here," she mumbles, stumbling to the corn stalks that are taller than Lucas.

We all get out of the car, and Lucas follows right behind her. Hannah hunches over and groans. "It's already been almost 15 minutes since we left the house," Hannah says. She looks around frantically and says, "It's getting worse every minute. I didn't even realize I was shot. I should've known. I can't…" Her eyes close, and she starts to fall backwards. Lucas grabs her hand and brings her back to the car.

"It's ok. It's going to be ok," he says, putting her back in the passenger seat. Her eyes flicker, and she flinches.

"It's getting worse," she whispers again. Lucas puts the car in reverse, a tear streaming down his face. He quickly wipes it away and starts driving.

"I know it's not a great time Lucas, but we're going like 65 miles an hour, and trees are starting to come up ahead. It's dangerous!" Henry says.

"Everyone," Hannah whispers. We're all quiet. "If you bring me back to camp, then there's no chance of getting the treasure. The counselors will take the treasure or just lock us in a cabin. Please think of the treasure."

"The treasure isn't going anywhere. I just want you to be okay," Lucas says, and they look deeply at each other.

"Listen, I know this is a long shot, but I know someone who can help her," Kim says. "There won't be any doctors arriving at camp once we get there for around an hour anyway. I know a man who used to be a doctor but lives on this lake somewhere."

"Somewhere?" Oliver raises his eyebrows at her.

"That's not a bad idea, but where is he?" I say, turning to Kim.

"He's my godfather, Dr. Crow. He'll be willing to help. He lives... let me remember...on the east side of the lake, so take a left!" Kim shouts and Lucas swerves around a stop sign.

"I'm going to die," Hannah says really softly.

"Don't say that," Lucas tells her.

"This route will only take longer," I say.

"But it's our only option," Kim says

"It takes at least 10 minutes to drive to the east side of the lake," Oliver calculates in his head and watches his GPS.

"Then let's take a shortcut," Lucas says, turning straight into the woods.

"What are you doing?!" Audrey yells.

"Taking a shortcut," Lucas repeats, dodging a tree.

"We're still going like 55!" Henry screams. "In the middle of the woods!"

"Watch out!" Kim yells as a deer runs past the car. Lucas sighs and keeps driving.

"There! That's it. That's my godfather's house," Kim says as Lucas pulls slanted into the driveway.

"Quick, get Hannah in there!" Oliver says.

Lucas helps Hannah over to the door, and Kim knocks three times.

"No ones home!" a voice says from inside.

"It's me Kim! You have to let us in!"

The door opens a crack, and a man with a black beard appears. "What's going on?" he says.

"She's been shot. We need help," I say quickly.

"Come in, come in." Blood is streaming down Hannah's leg now, and she leans into Lucas.

"It isn't her foot, is it? Cause I don't do foots." Lucas shakes his head as we walk past a small kitchen and living room. We turn down the hall into a sun-facing room, but the sun is behind trees, so it's dim. Lucas lays Hannah on the table, and she closes her eyes and winces.

"You know I'm not a surgeon, right?" Dr. Crow says. He's wearing thick glasses that don't exactly fit his face and a tropical shirt and shorts. We nod at his question. "This kind of deep injury requires me to go in and get the bullet out. I can't promise she'll wake up if I do the surgery, but it's our best and only chance."

We nod again. "Okay then, let's go in." Dr. Crow adds, "You can tell me how this happened later." He takes a tray of tools from a drawer. He points a sharp knife-like tool at Hannah's bloody stomach.

"Don't you have to wash the tools first?" Oliver asks frantically.

"Yes, yes." The suspicious doctor mutters and fumbles with the tool, quickly cleaning it. "She's lost a lot of blood, and we can't promise anything." Lucas nods again, like he's afraid he'll hurt Hannah if he talks. Dr. Crow gives Hannah an IV in her arm full of pain medicine, and I watch him carefully, not completely trusting this doctor.

Dr. Crow gets closer to Hannah, pressing for the wound. "Wait, it's in her hip. We're lucky the bullet didn't hit her stomach and other organs...or she'd already be dead." Dr. Crow stitches the red opening near Hannah's hip bone. "After I stitch her up all the way, watch over her. She's lost just over a pint of blood. That's a lot to lose, and there's no way of telling if she'll wake up."

The doctor finishes sewing Hannah and refills the IV. "Hey, pass me the whiskey," he says and Lucas grabs a bottle from the side table for him. "Thanks." He takes a swig, then splashes Hannah's wound to disinfect it. He focuses on his patient. "All done," Crow says after a few minutes of silence. He takes a step back to examine his work.

"What now?" Lucas asks, voice strained and face ghostly pale.

Crow looks at him with squinted eyes and says, "We wait."
And he walks into the hallway, the whiskey bottle in his hand.

Chapter 21

Prayers

Lucas

"We've waited for two hours," I say, not amused by this so-called "doctor." Crow is eating Flamin' Hot Cheetos on his couch, watching football.

"This guy is a loon," Oliver whispers.

"Y'all know that kind of job costs over $5,000 dollars or more, right?" Crow says, briefly looking up from the game.

We all squirm, and my eyes meet Kim's. She tilts her head just a little bit, and I understand at once, so I nod. Kim walks up to Crow and hands him the pure gold box the last map piece was in. "This is a pure gold chest, and if you don't believe me, ask the pawn shop down in Duluth. Pure. Gold," she tells her godfather.

"Holy crap! I'm rich!" he jumps off the couch, Cheetos flying everywhere.

A tunnel of thoughts swirl in my head. What if we didn't make it here in time to save Hannah? What if she's already dead? What if…everything is my fault?

"I'm going to check on Hannah," I say to everyone. Crow is just opening and closing the box over and over and over.

"Yeah yeah," he mutters, clearly not listening.

I turn down the hall away from the others still sitting there praying. I turn the door handle and push it open. Hannah's lying there, motionless, on the table. Ever since we met at the fence, I knew I liked her a lot, but I never thought she'd come on this adventure and that it would get her so hurt! Look at these innocent people who are risking their lives! For me. For the treasure.

I turn off my brain and walk up to Hannah. Her eyes are closed. She's barely breathing. Her IV machine is making noises. Beep, beep, beep, beep, beep, beep, beeeeeeeeeeeeeeeeeeeeeeeeeeep.

"Doctor Crow! Come in here! She's not breathing!" I scream, checking her not beating pulse. "Noooooo! Hannah, Hannah, stay with me!" I'm crying now.

The others are crowding the room, telling Hannah it's ok. Her eyes are still closed, and her heart is still not beating. Crow gives her CPR for a few minutes, then says it's worthless by now, but I keep going. Keep crying. Keep telling Hannah it's gonna be ok. "Stay with me, please!" I say, the others sitting in the chairs around the room praying and crying.

Oliver keeps saying it's an alternate universe and none of us are real. Henry sobs into his hands. Celia has her knees pulled to her chin, turning motionless. Kim is wiping her glasses, which are foggy and wet from crying. Audrey stays strong with her body language, but there's a lot of sadness in her eyes. And I...I'm mad, mad at Conner, mad at God, mad at the universe, mad at this lunatic of a doctor, mad at myself.

I grab an empty chair and throw it across the room. I turn around to see lifeless Hannah one more time and then punch the wall.

"Lucas, you can't run from this; you can't leave the rest of us. We're a family, like Hannah said," Audrey says. "A member of our family just...just died."

I keep hitting the wall until my fist stings. It's no use. They file out of the room, getting ready to leave. Leave this room, this house, this woods, this camp, this adventure, this treasure, this friendship. Nothing good ever lasts.

Beep, beep, beep, beep, beep, beep, beep, beep, beep. "Lucas?" Hannah's eyes flicker open. She sits up, and I run over to her.

"You're alive!" I exclaim quietly.

"Yeah, of course I am," she whispers.

"I was so worried, I thought you didn't make it," I say, shaking my head in disbelief. I almost lost her. We're so close, our faces inches apart. "Um...you remember before Conner broke in? We...we almost..." I don't finish my sentence before she kisses me. It feels a thousand times better than any kiss before all of this happened.

"Where are the others?" she asks, looking around.

"Oh, out there," I say, gesturing toward the door.

"We need to go get the treasure," she says, standing up.

"Hannah, you really shouldn't be walking yet." She falls backward, and I catch her for the second time in the past two days.

"If we wait any longer, we won't get the treasure on time. Counselors or someone will find us and bring us back to camp." She has her arm around my neck, and I'm helping her walk back to the others. "It hurts *a lot*. But I'll be ok, Lucas." They all gasp when we enter the living room.

"Hannah!" Oliver exclaims, throwing his hands in the air.

"We thought you were dead," Kim says, smiling with watery eyes behind her glasses.

"Seriously girl, you had me scared!" Celia flings her arms around her.

"Thanks everyone. We need to get going," Hannah says determinedly. We thank Dr. Crow, who is playing peekaboo with the gold box.

CHAPTER 22

REUNION

Audrey

I end up driving the car back to Ben's because two newly found "love birds" have been kissing in the back seat.

We drive for a few miles when Lucas starts talking instead. "Think about all we've been through, guys. Celia nearly got electrocuted by the fence and almost drowned in quicksand. Henry was about to eat a poison berry. Kim twisted her ankle. Oliver wrestled a snake and got sucked into a pitch black hole. Audrey almost got suffocated by a snake. And Hannah got shot! How has nothing bad happened to me yet?" He whistles. "I mean, I got all of you into this mess, I might as well get you out." We all cheer.

"The key word to that was *almost*, Lucas. I *almost* ate a poison berry!" Henry says. We all cheer again.

"Hey, got any more of that lemonade?" Oliver asks. We laugh, and I toss him the nearly empty can. We talk and enjoy being worry free for a while again, especially since we're so relieved that Hannah survived.

We arrive at Ben's house to see two cop cars sitting there. "What the heck? Why are the cops still here? It's been almost five hours since we left," I say.

We sneak out of the car and walk to the side of the shop. Then we jump into the window well. We watch the cops looking for something, and Ben is nowhere to be seen.

"What are they doing?" Hannah whispers.

"I don't know, but they're searching around," Kim says.

"Whisper!" we all command in a whisper.

"Maybe they found out about the treasure," Lucas whispers.

"How?" I say quietly.

"I don't know, but we can't stay here waiting for someone to find us and drag us back to camp," Hannah says.

"Then where do we go?" Oliver asks.

"Crow?" Kim suggests.

"No!" We all accidentally yell at once, and then the police are onto us. The bigger cop turns around and spots seven kids sitting in a window well.

"Run!" Lucas screams.

"We can't take Ben's car. What if *he* needs to run?" Kim yells.

"We have to! It's our only way out!" I say as we pile back into the car, Lucas driving this time.

"Kids! Get out of the vehicle right now!" the cops holler, now running at us.

"Punch it!" Oliver says. Lucas backs out of there at 30 miles an hour and hits the road at over 50.

"Dude faster!" Henry screeches in Lucas's ear.

"We're running out of gas; we can only go maybe 15 more miles," Lucas says. The gas gauge was low when I was driving, I think. Great.

"Crow's house is 10 miles away?" Kim suggests.

"I don't know; that man is completely crazy, but he did save Hannah's life," I say.

"We're running out of options!" Oliver says.

"Fine. Crow's it is," Lucas says.

"Ugh...ouch!" Hannah yelps.

"Oh yeah, Crow said once the pain killer wears off, it's going to be as bad as it gets!" Henry tells her.

"Well that explains it," Hannah says stiffly.

"I'm just glad you didn't die back there," Lucas says, and they look at each other dreamily.

"Uhh guys, sorry to break up this reunion, but the cops are coming!" Henry yells.

"Left!" Kim shouts from the seat in front of me. We turn into the woods at the perfect time. The cops zoom past on the main road. Lucas lets out a sigh of relief.

"Now what?" Oliver asks while we careen through trees. But the car soon sputters. We all get out to pull the car out of sight.

"This car is officially out of gas," Lucas says, leaning against the car door. We'll get it back to Ben later somehow.

We hike toward the shack of a house Crow lives in. I knock and no one answers. "Don't come in!" Crow's scratchy voice warns.

Lucas opens the door slowly, and I jump back a little. "What happened?" I mutter.

The house/shack is turned upside down. The dining table is flipped, glass is all over the floor, dirt from an indoor garden is on the walls, and the whole place is destroyed.

"I, I, I, was w-w-watching football when the g-ghost came through my house. It said something about returning the-the treasure back to where it belonged," Dr. Crow stutters as he's curled up on the floor.

"A ghost. Really?" Henry says, raising an eyebrow.

But I notice Hannah's body goes rigid. She crosses her arms, and her face is pale.

"Y-y-y-yes," Crow mutters. I hear a door slam upstairs. A chill runs down my arms as I fly back a few feet, nearly knocking Kim over.

"It's just the wind. When did this happen?" Oliver asks.

"Right after you left," he says, now using his normal tone. He's calming down.

"We need you to tell us everything," Lucas says.

"Well, I was driving back from the pawn shop, where they told me it *was* real gold, when I glanced in the rear view mirror and noticed I really needed to shave this beard." Crow scratches his neck. "So, I get home and I open the door and my place is trashed. I think someone must have broken in! I start to clean up the mess when I think what the heck, I'll do it after I shave."

Crow rambles, "So I walked into the bathroom, and I didn't shower or anything, but the mirror was fogged up and had words written on it. It said, *Return what you have taken to where it belongs.* I wrack my brain for things I've stolen in my life, and I can only think of one thing: the Snickers bar I stole from my brother when I was seven. Well, that's long gone in some sewage pipes now." He chuckles. "Then I think, how did that even get on my mirror; I didn't do it, so it must have been a ghost! Spirits *are* real! So I ran into the kitchen and dropped to the ground. Ever since, I've been laying here curled up on the floor and terrified the ghost will eat me," he finishes. "I'll show you!" He leads us to the bathroom.

"And you're sure it's a ghost?" Kim asks, squinting her eyes at the foggy writing on the bathroom mirror.

"What else could it b-b-be?" Crow stammers.

"I don't know," Kim says. "Maybe some robbers were messing with you?"

"We'll figure this out later, but right now the cops are after us," Hannah says sternly. She's still pale and seems weird ever since Crow started talking about ghosts.

"Take my car," Crow says, casually handing us the keys.

"Really?" I ask.

"Oh yeah, you kids crash and burn it for all I care. I could buy at least two new cars with this gold box you gave me," he says. I glance at Celia and exchange a critical look.

"Ok, thank you," Kim says, quickly taking the keys and walking out the door.

"Camp Honey Bear was rumored to be haunted. But it couldn't have been a real ghost, right?" Henry asks nervously.

"Doubt it," Celia says.

CHAPTER 23

A First Sign

Kim

"I know my godfather's crazy, but he wouldn't just lie about something like this. Basically, we have two options here: we figure out what we need to return, return it to the ghost and then *bam,* he's satisfied. Or we just forget about it all together and let Crow live in fear," I say in the backseat of the red, huge 1969 Chrysler convertible my godfather spent more money on than his own house. I see Hannah look down and she starts fidgeting.

"I vote for the second option. Besides, we have more important things to do than sit around telling fake ghost stories," Celia says.

Crash! What looks like a huge branch falls where Celia was sitting, before the car started driving! Hannah gasps. Everyone is completely still, the car practically driving itself while Lucas stares into where we were parked seconds ago. In Crow's driveway lies an entire oak tree.

"I think you made the ghost mad," Henry says to Celia, who has her hand over her mouth.

We keep driving in silence for a while when Henry says, "Guys, I gotta make a quick pit stop." We all glance at him.

"Whatever dude, just hurry up," Lucas says, unlocking the door.

"Just don't wipe with a leaf! Poison Ivy isn't the most pleasant thing to have on your butt," Oliver says. He tosses him a sock lying on the floor of the car, and I scrunch up my nose and close my eyes.

"Now that you mention it, I haven't gone in like a day," Hannah says, getting out of the car.

"Pee break!" Oliver shouts as we all exit the car.

"Girls on the left side of the road, boys on right," Audrey declares. We part with the boys and walk into the trees on the left of the road.

Minutes pass, and Celia says, "Wow, we've been through so much. I'm glad you're okay, Hannah!"

Hannah smiles. "Me too! I don't even want to think about getting shot or Conner or anything bad." She shudders. "It's so nice to relax for a bit…"

"And enjoy some girl time and nature," I agree.

Celia says, "It's also kind of nice being away from the boys, isn't it? I mean, they're cool and all, but sometimes you just wanna talk girl to girl."

"I guess," Hannah says, peering over at the boys chasing each other around with sticks.

"Girl! I just said it's nice to be *away* from the boys, not to constantly be staring at them!" Celia teases, sitting on a log covered in moss.

"Sorry, sorry, I just...there's something exciting about being in a relationship, but it's scary because when you have something so great, you don't want to lose it," Hannah says, turning to face the three of us on the log.

I take Hannah's hands and squeeze them when I tell her, "Hannah, if it doesn't last for whatever reason, you know it's just not meant to be. Not like I'm saying it's not, but if you like Lucas so much, you should get to know him better so you can get along better." I smile. "You've only known him for a week. Four days at camp and three not at camp. You're only going to get closer." I can tell Lucas really likes her, and I'm kind of over him anyway. We weren't compatible like he and Hannah are, and I'm only 13 anyway, I think.

"Guys look! Those flowers are beautiful!" Audrey says, pointing over at a patch of wildflowers.

"Wow!" Celia says. We run over and fall onto the soft grass. I roll onto my belly and pick the little daisy in front of my nose.

I stick it behind my ear, and Audrey says, "Hey, when I was little, I made these crowns out of flowers. Maybe we could make them?"

I start to daydream about shimmering gold crowns that could possibly be found in the treasure. But I quickly snap out of my daze and start to gather the prettiest flowers we can find and make a pile of them. Celia makes a crown of sticks and leaves and another of sticks and flowers. She sets the flower one on my head, and I curtsy. She puts the other in her pocket.

We laugh and talk about girl things, nothing like in the Volvo. About 10 minutes pass by, and we all wear our flower crowns and can't stop laughing for no reason on the grass.

Chapter 24

Pure Bad Luck

Henry

"Hey Lucas?" I ask him.

"Yeah?" he says.

"Are you gonna ask Hannah to be your girlfriend?" I've been wondering this ever since they almost kissed.

"I don't know; I guess if she wants to be," he replies with a shy smile. "Oliver, don't you have something going with Celia?" Lucas stands up to walk to the little stream a few feet away.

"I mean I like her, but I can't tell if she even remotely can tell. Or if she likes me at all," Oliver says hopelessly and walks over to Lucas sitting by the stream.

"You gotta get her attention somehow or tell her you think she's great," I say, sitting down between them on the leafy ground.

"He's right, man; go get her! Like I did with Hannah, and it went pretty well for me," Lucas says, and Oliver grins, then stands up and begins to walk across the road into the girls' territory.

"Wish him luck," Lucas says to me as Oliver hurries off. "He's gonna need it."

I laugh. "Yeah he does." I clear my throat. "About that ghost thing, I feel like we should just forget about it. It's kind of stupid to dwell on it like Crow, don't you think?"

"Duck!" Lucas yells, his eyes big with fear.

"Duck? Where?" I ask, confused.

"No, duck down!" Lucas yells again. I do as he said, and I hear this nasty buzzing noise above me. I look up, expecting to see a bee, so I brace myself. Swarming my whole body is about 40 wasps! Not just one bee! I swat at them and race toward the car.

"Girls, run! There are wasps!" I scream, and a shadow of five people runs toward me. The wasps start stinging. Like a lot. My entire face and body are aching and burning. I feel bumps forming all over my neck and upper body. It feels like I'm burning in a bonfire.

"Start the car, Lucas, please!" I try to say, but my lips have been stung, and maybe so has my tongue.

I feel my face blowing up like a balloon, and I hear Audrey yell, "He's allergic! I've seen this before, and soon it'll be hard for him to breathe. Lucas, hurry!"

The car starts to move, and the wasps clear out. I see none of the others got as badly stung as I did–just a few minor patches of red on some of their legs and arms.

"Henry, it's ok. We're getting you to a doctor," Kim says. I can see out of my not-stung eye, and the girls are crying, telling Lucas to move faster.

"Where do we go? Crow won't be any help cause he's a nervous wreck, so he won't know how to treat it," someone says.

It's getting harder to see and hear things. I feel someone holding my not-inflated hand. It's hard to breathe. I manage to say, "EPI pen."

And Oliver unzips his pouch and pulls one out. "How could I forget I had one of these?" he says.

"Hurry up! He can't breathe!"

"Oliver, you don't need to zip the pouch back up. He needs it!"

"Hang on, Henry!" I feel something sharp go into my arm, and I can't hold my eyes open any longer.

CHAPTER 25

RUSTIC GOLD

Celia

"I think Henry's gonna be asleep for a while," I say, peering across the room at Henry peacefully sleeping on a big, brown leather chair in Ben's living room. His light auburn hair is messier than usual. Ben sits in an armchair beside him, promising he will watch over Henry. He has the TV on quietly while he rocks in the chair.

I smile and quickly follow the others down the creaky, old stairs to Ben's basement. Looking around, I get a strange vibe, and I don't know what it is.

Lucas walks over to the Big Dipper painting on the wall. He told us the painting was hollow in the back, Hannah agreed that the hollowness in the back could maybe lead to a room behind the painting and maybe even the treasure. Plus, it was smart to come back to Ben's so Henry could rest, and Ben was more than happy to let us inside to keep searching for the treasure. He thankfully handed Conner over to the cops a while ago.

Lucas sighs. "Are you ready for the moment we've all been waiting for?" He starts to grasp the large painting on the wall, and I hold my breath. Kim bites her lip so hard, it turns white, and Oliver is closing his eyes. Lucas keeps pulling at the painting, but it doesn't move.

"Here, let me," I say, and Lucas steps to the side as I look closer at the painting. On the left side of the frame are two small golden clasps, like on a door. I dig my nails behind the right side until I feel a handle. Pulling it too hard might break it off, so I gently lift it. Worked like a charm! The whole painting opens up to reveal a dark hole in the wall behind it.

"Well done!" Lucas looks a bit astonished that he didn't realize the door mechanism himself. I hold my head high as I take a step forward to look inside.

"Oh my gosh," Audrey mutters, and climbs inside the decently big hole. The others follow. All sorts of rustic things are scattered around the room. The window in Ben's basement is quite big, so it provides a warm tone of light streaming in on the peeling flower wallpaper.

"What is all of this?" Hannah asks, picking up the map and handing it to Lucas.

"I don't know," he replies, looking disappointed there is no treasure back here.

To be honest, I was expecting a treasure too. Speaking of, a little bit of shine and shimmer catches my eye.

I reach for a rustic, gold spyglass tucked behind a box full of wool coats and wooden shoes. Every item in the room has layers of dust. I let out a sneeze, inhaling some of it. Examining the spy glass, I realize it has a name carved in the side, "Maria Rennald, 1632?" I say aloud. *Could this be the woman who buried the treasure?*

"Huh?" Audrey says. She looks over my shoulder at the spyglass. "Who could that be?"

Sweat forms on my forehead. None of this makes sense. *Pirates* buried the treasure, not this lady. My throat goes dry when I whisper, "I don't know."

CHAPTER 26

EXPECT THE UNEXPECTED

Celia

Everyone stares at the dusty telescope that's the size of my hand. "I bet it's nothing," Lucas says, walking over to a few wooden boxes in the corner in search of other clues.

I nod at his explanation but put the spyglass in my pocket–just in case Lucas was wrong about it. Pushing my hair behind my ears, I start digging through some of the dusty stuff.

"I never thought we'd be finding things this old! Like over four hundred years kind of old!" Kim says, holding up a brown, wool coat that smells like cottage cheese.

"Yeah, me neither," I agree, wrinkling my nose at the smell. I take the spyglass out of my pocket and turn it around in my hand.

"This is not where I thought we would end up! A couple of days ago, I thought we would just find the treasure buried in the ground, take our riches, and go back home," Lucas starts rambling.

"But nooo, we have to look through this ancient guy's stuff who died over three centuries ago!"

We all turn and look at him, my lips in a straight line. Shifting my feet, I try to find a distraction from this awkward moment. *Lucas has lost it,* I think, casually walking across the musty, cobweb-filled room.

I turn around after sitting on one of the wooden boxes to see Hannah comforting Lucas. I can tell he's very disappointed about not finding the treasure.

A sudden pain shoots through my limbs as the wood box I was sitting on breaks, and I come crashing through the bottom. "Ouch," I mutter, rubbing my newly bruised back.

"You ok?" Kim asks, giving me a hand.

This gives me deja vu of when I didn't help Kim up when we crashed into each other toward the start of camp. I cringe, my heart breaking. How could I be so rude without even realizing it? At least I helped with her twisted ankle in the cave. Taking Kim's hand, I get up and say, "Yeah I'm good."

"Hey, what's that?" Audrey asks, and I turn my gaze to where her finger is pointing.

In the place I was just sitting, underneath all of the wood splinters and pieces, is a journal. It's made of thick paper and has a leather cover with an engraved tree in the center. I hear the others talking about the journal, but something about it draws me in. Like I can't stop staring at it. This odd sensation runs through my body, like a wave from the ocean.

Finally, Hannah reaches out and picks up the intriguing journal. We all circle around her and the sturdy pages.

She turns from the cover to the first page. A shiny, little silver locket sits in the back cover. Written in neat cursive on the paper is:

This journal belongs to Christopher R. Rennald

My mouth opens to say something, but nothing comes out. *"Rennald?"* Hannah mutters, her eyes widening like a thought just hit her. "That same last name was on the spyglass. I think it's all connected," she adds.

My mouth falls open, and I grab the journal. I turn to the next page and start to read the small, cursive ink words, but before I can make out the first sentence, something very strange happens.

The words start to blur and swirl together like a whirlpool of jumbled writing. The smell of sea salt starts to fill the air, and my feet are lifted off the floor! My whole body seems to be made of liquid, and when I turn to look at my hand it's a stringy glob of color. I start to panic, but I'm falling through the air! The world around me turns to a long, endless spiral with cream colored pages of a story…or a journal, fluttering all around me. The pages fall light and graceful like snow on a winter's day. Hundreds and hundreds of them.

I start flaring around in fear, but then my feet touch the ground! A long and wide wood dock stretches under me like it's just been built. A scene begins to form around me. I hear ocean waves crashing on the shore and peoples' voices, the smell of freshly baked bread in the air. I'm on a...*boardwalk?* I frantically look around for the others, but they're nowhere to be seen.

Scurrying behind a large box, I hear a young boy's voice say, "This is all I have, but you can take it." I turn quickly to see a woman wearing ragged clothes and a boy around the age of seven or eight standing in front of her, wearing a torn up, dirty pair of pants and shirt and a hat with two large holes in it.

"This can buy us a meal for one," the woman says in a kind, gentle voice, "but we will share." The boy nods and sits down on a barrel a little bigger than he is, holding the journal under his arm. Just then, the scene changes.

Now, I'm on a dock, but it's smaller and doesn't have nearly as many people coming by. Can the people see me? I notice sailors all around, boarding ships and carrying fish nets, and barrels of things. Then I see the boy, only much older. Sixteen or seventeen maybe?

The boy is talking to a man who yells in a scratchy voice, "I told you how many times! You can not sail a ship unless you have the money!" He pauses. "I am sorry Christopher; I don't make the rules. Now run off and have your lunch."

So he *is* Christopher from the first page of the journal! Christopher starts to walk in my direction, kicking a rock off the edge of the wooden dock with a splash. He can't see me, right?

"Hello," he says to me with a smile.

I inhale sharply, my eyes widening, "Um hi."

"Funny clothes you're wearing! I like them."

"Oh yeah," I reply, looking down at my plaid romper.

"You are not from here, are you?" he asks, looking at me like I'm some sort of gem.

"No, no. I'm not from here."

What is going on?! One minute I'm in the present day, and the next I'm somewhere in the 1600's talking to *Christopher* himself!

"Why don't I show you around? Buy us some food."

My eyebrows shoot up. *Is he asking me out? What do I say? I mean, any second the scene is going to change again!*

"Sure." I gulp and follow Christopher, who is starting to walk ahead. Catching up to him, I ask, "Have you lived here your whole life?"

"You do talk funny too! Yes, I have lived here my whole life. Nothing quite like the ocean air."

I nod, slowly processing what's happening. Christopher walks up to a food stand and gets us each a piece of homemade bread. "Thanks," I tell him, biting into the soft, buttery goodness.

We sit on the beach, eating bread and talking. For a hot second, I almost forget where I am and what I'm doing. Christopher's curly black hair and deep brown eyes catch my breath. Am I seriously falling for a boy who is dead in my time? "You have very beautiful eyes," he says, tucking one of my blonde curls behind my ear.

"Thank you," I mumble as he pulls me in for a kiss. Suddenly, the scene changes.

I want to cry! Can I please go back for just one minute?! The ocean sand disappears, and now I'm back on wood. Accept not a wooden dock…a wooden ship.

"I can't believe I saved enough to have *this* for my work! I have waited my whole life for this moment," someone on the ship says. I can tell it's Christopher's voice. "It is very important that we were chosen to sail the gift of peace to the queen in London. My mother would be proud." Christopher looks sad but immediately brushes it away when he says, "What do you sailors talk about when you're at sea for a long time?" I hide behind a barrel, tempted to run back to him.

"We talk about our families, the ship, the ocean, women," the other sailor says to Christopher, who is steadily steering the wheel. I notice he has grown a beard. He might be twenty five or thirty? "Did you ever love a woman? Other than your wife of course."

Christopher takes a deep breath, "When I was about seventeen, I met a girl. She was peculiar but also very pretty. The day I met her, we sat by the shore and talked for hours. Then I leaned in to kiss her and the second our lips touched, she vanished into thin air!"

Every inch of me wants to yell out, *"Christopher, I'm right here!"* But I can't. I'll just vanish again.

"We're closing in on the Bahamas for a rest!" a crewman shouts from the crow's nest above. *The vacation islands?* I think.

Before Christopher or anyone can respond, I hear yelling. There are men dressed in all black running across the ship with swords and knives in their hands. Everything happens so fast, it's a blur. Screaming, clashing, fire, blood, bombs. Then everything is over. Any man who isn't dressed in all black is either dead or injured.

Tears fill my eyes as I watch the battle. I would try to help, but I know I can't be seen, or else bad things that I can't explain will start to happen. I don't want to mess up time or history.

My heart jumps at the thought of Christopher lying dead somewhere on the ship. But then I see him. He's escaping on a small wooden raft like boat. I sigh in relief…and it all disappears again.

As quickly as the scene dissolves, another comes to life.

"I am so delighted you are home!" a young woman's voice says happily.

Just like that, I'm on the first floor of Ben's shop. But it's a very old house in this version, which is weird.

"As am I, Catherine," Christopher says. I hide behind a fireplace, which is very warm. The smell of burnt logs is strong because I'm so close to the rusty, old thing.

"Father, look at what I have painted!" A small girl around the age of nine comes to him with a large piece of art I recognize, being the one we opened and climbed through in Ben's basement, while he was running errands.

"Tis beautiful, Maria! We will be sure to put it up on the empty wall downstairs," older-looking Christopher says, taking the starry painting and hanging it on the wall in the basement. I follow quietly to make sure I'm not spotted.

"Ouch!" I mutter, hitting the fireplace as I get up. Luckily, it didn't burn me, but the metal made a clanking noise.

"What was that?!" Catherine exclaims from downstairs.

"I will go see, Mother," Maria says, running up the stairs. She finds me right away. I panic and freeze as Maria and I stare at each other for a moment. "Who are you?" Maria whispers slowly, her eyebrows furrowed as she looks at my romper. "And what are you wearing?"

"My name is Celia, but it's very hard to explain how and why I'm here. To be honest, I don't even know why or how," I whisper frantically, hoping Maria's parents don't come up. "*Please* don't tell your mom and dad. Just trust me."

"I shall not tell them," Maria says, her eyes wide.

"I think this belongs to you," I say and hand her the golden spyglass from my pocket. She takes it carefully and turns to leave. "Oh, and my outfit is called a romper. Be the one who invents them."

She smiles at me and goes back downstairs for real. I hear her through the floorboards. "It was only the fireplace again," Maria says.

Then, almost in a flash, I'm downstairs in the room behind the painting. I slide my way behind one of the bigger boxes and watch as Christopher climbs through the hole behind the painting, the journal in his hand. His hair is graying, and so is his beard. *It's so strange seeing him grow up in such a short amount of time!*

A much older Catherine quickly follows, holding teenage Maria's hand. They are both crying and muttering things to each other. "Stay here until tomorrow. By then, the pirates will be gone," Christopher says, hugging his wife and daughter. "If I do not return…well…know that I love you both dearly."

He runs his hand over the journal and gently sets it inside the wood box I broke earlier. Currently, it's still intact. *All of this time stuff is confusing me!* I think. But the pirates are chasing him down. Poor Christopher. They must think he still has the treasure from the ship.

Christopher closes the box, climbs back out of the room, and closes the painting behind him. I sigh, feeling awful for Catherine and Maria.

Just then, a thought hits me like a train. *How can I tell the others that the treasure is really washed up on the shores of the Bahamas if I'm stuck in the past?* If Christopher was sailing near the islands and those assassins sunk the ship when they bombed it, then it has to be there!

Racking my brain for any ideas, I see a blank piece of paper tucked under a box. I grab it so quickly, I give myself a little papercut. I start to write a message (with the blood from my papercut) to give to my friends. It's absolutely disgusting, but it's my only option! The message reads:

Oliver, Lucas, Hannah, Kim, Audrey, and Henry,

You're probably freaking out because I'm somehow in the journal! Go to the Bahamas! The treasure is there. Bring the journal along because I'm obviously trapped inside. Hope you get this! Love Celia, from centuries ago :)

I fold the paper into a small square and slowly open the box where Christopher put the journal. Carefully, I tuck the note near the end of the journal's pages and close the box tightly. Now I wait.

CHAPTER 27

WHAT HAVE I MISSED?

Henry

I open my eyes and wipe drool from the side of my mouth. I'm on a brown leather couch. I sit up and feel my face. It deflated! That's a good sign. I see we're not in the convertible anymore, and there are thankfully no wasps.

I think I hear voices from downstairs, and Ben checks me over to make sure I'm alright. He then tells me that the others are searching in the basement. I hurry downstairs and glimpse everyone through a hole behind a painting on the wall.

I climb through the painting to find my friends. "Where is the treasure?" I ask, confused. All I see are dusty old boxes…but wait…Hannah is holding a journal, and everyone is crowded around her. The pages move by themselves, and I nearly pass out again.

"He's awake! The treasure isn't here, but we found a message from Celia in the back of the journal! Oh, and a heart locket in the journal's back cover too," Kim says, hugging me.

Hannah lifts the locket necklace's chain, pulling it from under her shirt to show me. It's a metal heart-shaped locket with little swirly engravings, the kind that clicks open and holds pictures. My mom has one like it. "It's really stuck, so we can't get it open to tell if it's a clue, but here it is," Hannah says. "I'll keep wearing it to keep it safe," she adds. I nod.

"Cool. Can I have a mirror?" I ask. Audrey hands me a compact. I click it open; I look like I have a million chickenpox all over my body, but I know they're wasp stings. "How bad is it really?" I ask Oliver.

"I guess you've been worse, but it's just a minor inconvenience to our treasure expedition," Oliver replies.

"What do you mean? What have I missed?" I ask. "And where's Celia? What message?"

"I *mean* we're going to be in the middle of the ocean soon," Oliver says casually. "We'll explain in the car."

CHAPTER 28

HISTORY

Oliver

After we've left the room, crowded into Crow's car, and explained the entire history of the treasure and that Celia is still somehow in the magical journal on Hannah's lap, Henry yells, "What?!" The engine of Crow's ruby red convertible hums as Ben merges onto the highway, the forest of tall trees surrounding us on both sides of the road.

"Yeah, a lot has happened since you've been asleep," Kim says to Henry. She holds up the note from Celia, and Henry reads it.

While we drive for hours with the top up and down, we catch Henry up on this long, difficult story. It's hard for him to believe the whole *being sucked into the journal and time traveling back to the year 1632* situation. But he and Ben know we have proof, with Celia's black and white comic-book-like picture still moving in the journal and her note that she signed. Ben never knew he had a secret room behind the painting either. He also left his souvenir shop with a sign that read *Closed for Vacation* so he could be gone for a while without questions.

"Sometimes you just need to have faith," Ben adds, and I nod. Though I love science, this journal, Celia's figure moving through it, and the note are odd time-traveling I can't deny.

"Now, back to Ben's shop. While we were finding the journal, Ben heard a news broadcast come on. It said, *Breaking News: a man named Conner Wills has broken out of jail!*" I tell Henry.

Lucas says, "Conner is out on the loose now, man, and he's trying to get the treasure!"

"But if the pirates Celia saw got the treasure, and they were last seen at the Bermuda Triangle, then that means," Henry says, frowning, "that the treasure would be washed up somewhere in the... *Bahamas.*" Henry shakes his head.

"Where do you think we're going now?" I say, leaning back in the car's plush seat, though there's little space. We're all squished together, but at least Ben's car has AC.

"We're driving to Rhode Island and then heading down to the Bahamas," Lucas says. "Ben has a friend with a big boat we can use."

"Do our parents know?" Henry asks.

"Nope!" Hannah says. "They still think we're at camp."

"And what were the police looking for in Ben's basement before?" Henry asks.

"The gun," Audrey says quietly.

"The gun Conner used to shoot Hannah. It fell in a crack in the floorboard," I tell him.

"Did they find it?" Henry asks.

"Yup, that's why he was in jail," Kim says.

"If I know Conner, I bet he's on his way to a different country where he isn't called a fugitive," Ben says. "Sorry again Hannah for the pain you went through," he adds sadly.

Hannah, in the front seat, smiles at Ben and tells him it's okay. She's survived so much, I think.

"But that country could be the Bahamas," Henry says.

"We know," Hannah says.

"Does Conner know about the journal or that the treasure could be in the Bahamas?" Henry asks.

"We don't know," Audrey says.

"Wait, when exactly did Conner break out?" Henry asks.

"Yesterday…the same day he was brought to the jail and you were stung by the bees. We're guessing he bribed one of the police to break him out," Lucas says.

"Wait a second, if the ghost wants us to bring the treasure to where it belongs, it would be with Christopher because the King and Queen of New England are dead. So the rightful person or place to give it to is where Christopher was buried," Henry says.

"What if we find his grave?" Lucas asks.

"No one gives a crap if we find it or not. The treasure is probably gonna be put in a museum...knowing people," Audrey says.

While the miles tick by in the car, I say, "Ok well that is a problem we didn't think of."

"Does anyone need to know though?" Hannah asks. Ben grins at her as he drives. "We can do whatever we want with the treasure, like give it back to a museum...or keep some for ourselves."

"I like how you think, Hannah!" Lucas says.

CHAPTER 29

REVEAL

Lucas

After hours on the road, a few pit stops for snacks and bathroom breaks, and too many games of *I Spy*, we finally make it to the coast. We meet Ben's nice friend and are sailing away, into the deep blue waves before I know it.

Sea spray rises up as I stand on the huge, metal boat's deck. It has a little captain's room, a roof, and a downstairs too. Like a mini cruise ship, I think.

"How does Ben know how to drive a boat this big?" Henry asks. I can feel the deck rock slightly, and I have to regain balance.

Audrey says from the prow, "He used to give tours around the Bahamas when he was younger, so he knows how to get there."

Suddenly, a fuzzy shape appears in front of me. The tiny, colorful particles start to form a person. Celia!

"You're back!" I shout. "But how did you–" My sentence is cut off by her voice.

"Ok, what is this your 50th question?" Celia says, "And yes I could hear all of you talking from in the journal."

"What was it like being trapped in the 1600's?" Kim asks, pushing her glasses up.

"I'll tell you guys everything, I promise," Celia says, grinning.

"And how long will this boat trip take?" Henry asks, completely out of the blue.

"Probably a few days," I say, my head spinning with questions. "All I can think of is this 'ghost of Christopher.' I mean how could it even be real? We're the rightful owners of this treasure if we find it. Guys, we've literally put blood, sweat, and tears into finding it, and now we either have to give it to a ghost or put it in a museum. No, I can't do that," I say looking out at the ocean waves. How could this happen? The others are just thinking too logically, right? I stand up and walk into the small room next to this one and sit down on a leather couch, the warm sunlight shining in.

"Hey, it's gonna be ok," Hannah says, grabbing my hand and squeezing it.

"But what if it's not? What if we're all risking our lives for a treasure that's not gonna be ours someday?" I ask, letting go of her hand.

"It's better than making crafts back at camp. Just think on the bright side. What did we all start out as? Wimpy camp nerds. Not anymore! We're stronger, braver, and tougher." Hannah smiles. "We just have to return this treasure back to Christopher, and then we won't have to keep risking getting killed! Again, maybe we can take some of the treasure for ourselves," Hannah says, sitting back on the couch next to me with her hands behind her head.

"Yeah ok," I say. "You're right. I've been so caught up with this treasure that I haven't really gotten to know you."

"Well, what do you wanna know?" Hannah asks, tilting her head.

"I'm just curious, like what's your favorite song or your middle name or your first pet?"

"Ummm…I like old songs like Elton John or the Beatles. My middle name is Rae, and my first pet was a butterfly named Cloudy," she says matter of factly.

"A butterfly named Cloudy?" I ask, laughing.

"Yes! We found him on a bush in the springtime when I was about five, and he was weak and had a broken wing, so we took him in and fed him sugar water. He eventually got back to his normal health and flew off. It was a sad day," she says.

"Well then, sorry I ever doubted you." We both laugh. "How about you? Same questions," she says.

I smirk at her. "I really like rock songs or instrumental guitar music, my middle name is John, and my first pet is my dog Penny, who is also my best friend."

When I finish talking, Hannah is sitting there smiling cutely at me. "Instrumental guitar?" she asks.

On instinct, I stand up, walk across the room, and pick up the acoustic guitar sitting in the corner. I noticed it on our first day on the boat. Sitting back down next to Hannah, I close my eyes and start to strum a melody. The melody turns into a smooth song that I remember off the top of my head. When I finish my unexpected guitar solo, Hannah is staring at me, astonished at my hidden talent. "That was *amazing,* Lucas!"

"I think I should teach you," I say, grinning.

Her eyes widen, and she shakes her head, "I…I can't play the guitar for the life of me."

"I haven't taught you yet," I whisper and slide down onto the carpeted floor.

I gesture for her to sit on the rug with me as I pull the guitar strap over my head. She moves in front of me, and I drape the strap over her shoulder and gently set the guitar in her lap.

I kneel over her and start to carefully curl her fingers into chords. My arms are around her body as she strums a C chord, then a G, then an F.

Soon enough, she is playing a melody. "You're doing great," I breathe, and she smiles up at me in agreement. "This will be one of our better adventures won't it?" I ask, smirking.

"Yes. Yes it will," Hannah responds, and she grins back at me.

She turns to me, shifting the guitar to her back. Her lips touch mine, and she cups my face in her soft, warm hands. She strokes my now messy hair, her pretty brown eyes catching my breath. We stay in a close embrace as I slip the guitar away from us. Soon, we're not talking anymore while our boat floats over the clear and open ocean.

CHAPTER 30

NIGHT PASSAGE

Catherine
July 4, 1955

The door of Cardinal Cabin creaks as I open it slowly, trying not to wake the other girls. I slip out and immediately feel the humid, summer night air warm my skin. Carefully, I close the door behind me and start to walk toward the forest.

"Cathy?" I whip around to see my best friend, Susie Marvin, standing behind me. "Where are you going?" she asks, and I sigh.

"All of the older kids and junior counselors are setting off fireworks at the Fourth of July party in the woods. I was just gonna check it out," I say, and her mouth falls open, but she quickly closes it and frowns.

Susie grabs my hand and starts to drag me back to our cabin. "No, no way," she says. "It's dangerous in the woods alone at night. And plus, you would get in so much trouble for this!" She's always been a good girl.

I struggle against her grip, pulling her so I can walk back to the woods. "This is where all the cool older kids go, Susie. There will be fireworks and all the Fourth of July celebrations! This is my chance! Besides, we're almost 12." She glares at me. "I'll be fine; just go back to the cabin and *stay there*. I don't want you getting in trouble because of me." I slip my hand from her and break into a run. I don't look back, even though Susie shouts my name.

I run faster, and I can't hear Susie coming after me any longer, so I assume she's gone back to bed. She never breaks the rules.

Sticks and leaves crunch under my feet as I sprint through the towering shadows of the woods. I finally stop to catch my breath and slam to a halt when the trees and bushes clear and I see the old cottage that kids at camp say is haunted. Some say they hear screaming coming from it, and there's even talk of a murder…of bodies thrown in the lake.

Of course, I never believed any of that nonsense and am prepared to prove them wrong. I can hear the loud music booming and cracking fireworks from here. They're bursting in the sky above the lake and reflecting colorfully from the sky into the water.

But instead of joining the fun and taking any chance of becoming one of the cool kids at this camp or being at an awesome party, I jump into the window well of the cottage. All of the lights are out in the house, so I assume nobody's home. Carefully, I slide in the open window and hop down onto the creaking floorboards of the basement. The strong stench of swampy-smelling water hits me. I find a flashlight nearby, grabbing it. I turn the flashlight on and shine it around the room. The basement is empty and covered with dust. A shiver runs down my spine, and I swallow the lump in my throat.

A drop of water falls onto my nose, and it somehow washes a sensation over me like a wave from the ocean, and I start to taste salt from the sea. The odd feeling goes away as quickly as it came, and I turn to face the wall. I wipe the drop of water off my nose, and a big painting covered in cobwebs catches my eye.

A weird latch on the right side of the frame makes me curious, so I pull it as hard as I can. The starry painting opens completely and leaves a big hole for me to climb through!

I swing my legs up and over into the hidden room behind the painting. As I shine my light around, a tall person standing in front of me makes me scream as loud as I can. I stumble forward and trip over a small box on the floor. I close my eyes tight and hope that the man standing there doesn't hurt me–or worse kill me.

I wait for what feels like years until I muster up enough courage to open my eyes and say, "Who's there?" I shine my flashlight right into the killer's eyes.

There's only one thing…he doesn't have eyes. Or a face or body. The "man" I was so afraid of was a coat hanging on a mannequin! Thank goodness!

I stand up and start to look around, only to find a bunch of old junk. I think that maybe there's something like an old artifact that's worth a lot of money though, so I open up some boxes. One small wooden box in particular, the box I tripped over, seems intriguing. I bend down and pick it up slowly, not wanting whatever's inside to break.

I open the box carefully to find an old-fashioned leather journal. Lifting the journal, my hands start to quiver, and the weird sensation comes back. Like the ocean waves again. I blow a thick layer of dust off the journal and open it up to the first page. After reading that the book belongs to Christopher Rennald, I turn the page.

But before I can read anything else, a gust of wind blows me backwards, and I drop the book. All the sudden, the forceful wind sucks me into the pages, and a swirl of light and color swallows me while I scream.

CHAPTER 31

PARADISE ISLAND

Celia

"Welcome to paradise," Ben says, stepping out of the captain's den and tying our boat up to a white dock.

"We're really here!" I say, looking out the window at the Bahamas. "We didn't exactly pack anything, so I've been wearing the same outfit for six days now!" I must be filthy, but then I realize that none of us have showered in like a week.

"The first thing I'm gonna do when I get to our hotel is take a nice, hot shower," Hannah says, sitting across from me on the boat, like she read my mind.

"I can't wait to charge my phone either," Audrey says. Audrey and Ben are the only ones with working phones left. Celia's phone and camera broke in the caves, as did Lucas's, and the rest of us left our phones in the cabins at camp…before our adventure really began.

We're all sitting at the coffee table in the boat's downstairs, eating our lunch: fish. All we've had for days straight is fish. Cooked fish, breaded fish, slimy fish, small fish. All fish. Most of them Ben caught. I'm dying to eat a home cooked meal. Other than fish. We finish our meal and all walk out to the deck.

"Cowabunga!" Oliver yells, cannonballing off the dock into the clear, turquoise blue water.

I laugh, and one by one we're all in the water. We don't have to wait to shower since we're basically taking a bath in the ocean, I think. The taste of salt on my tongue feels good and tropical. Other boats are lined up in a row. They're way nicer than ours too.

"Wooee! These babies are fancy. Cassy here is older than me. Wonder what all of those boats cost," Ben says, beaming at his friend's boat, which is painted with the name *Cassy* on the side.

"I smell something," I say, popping my head out of the water. I'm face to face with Audrey.

"Yeah it smells like," she sniffs the air, "Piña Coladas!"

Lucas shouts, and we all get out of the sand bar, sopping wet. Ben hands us each a ten dollar bill.

"Oh no, Ben, you don't have to," Kim says, looking at the money.

"Yeah really," Hannah says.

Henry and the boys are already buying their drinks at an oceanside stand, and us four girls are feeling awkward and apologetic. Ben looks very surprised.

"Once we find that treasure, we won't need cash. We'll have gold. So take it; it's my pleasure," Ben says. I nod and say thanks.

We all walk toward the stand where the boys are slurping their drinks. I order an alcohol-free twist of coconut and strawberry in my drink. The man behind the counter gives me a head nod and then starts preparing it by hand. I turn to talk with Hannah about what she's getting, but a flash of color catches my eye.

"Hey, look at those bikinis! I need one," I say, and start to run toward the little tent set up on the shoreline. I walk in, and the room lights up with color. Swimsuits, earrings, bracelets, tropical candies, surf boards, beach balls. Everything. The smell of sunscreen fills the air as I walk through my new favorite store.

"Hey, wait up!" Everyone else comes in, and we all smile.

"They have everything we need here!" Kim says, handing me my cold drink. I take a sip and taste paradise.

CHAPTER 32

BUSTED

Audrey

"Finally, some peace and quiet," I say, looking out at the crystal blue water. Henry and I are sitting on the beach while the others are swimming. Ben is off at the nearest historic monument in search of details about the treasure.

I glance at my phone, which is now beeping. I click on the red flashing circle. It leads me to a news report: "Seven lost kids! They disappeared one week ago today and have shown no sign of return. Former camp counselor Ben Wills is the suspect for either kidnapping or committing homicide to these innocent teens. Reward of $20,000 for finding Ben or children, alive or not! This is a dangerous man, so be careful. This is Century Scoop coming to you live from Minneapolis, Minnesota!" I gasp, along with Henry, who just saw the same thing.

"No," Henry mutters. I look back at my phone to see 42 missed calls from my parents. Oops.

"Guys, come look at this!" I call down to Hannah, Oliver, Lucas, Kim, and Celia. They're all splashing each other and laughing down in the ocean. Too busy having fun to notice.

"Henry, I need to go find Ben. This is really bad," I say, putting my shorts on over my swimsuit.

"I'm coming with you," Henry says, standing up, but I shake my head.

"Someone has to tell the others." I walk over to the town. "I have money; I'll figure things out," I say as Henry sits back down, looking shocked and nervous.

"It'll be ok. I know it will," I say, grabbing my flip flops and money.

Then, I start to walk down the busy street full of tourists and tents set up, their vendors selling all sorts of foods and souvenirs. Two cute, wild pigs cross my path as I'm walking. They give me a snort and then go off to the beach. I keep walking, determined to find Ben at some historic site around here. A group of boys wolf whistle in my direction. Embarrassed, I walk faster. Most of the other civilians and tourists seem normal. It's a bit nerve racking walking in a different country alone.

A tourist woman walks by, and I jump at the chance to say, "Hi, um do you know where the nearest museum or historic sight is?"

"The nearest museum would be the Rennald museum of sunken ships about ten miles north from here," the woman tells me, smiling.

"Ok, thank you!" I say, and run to the closest bus stop. I look at my $5 and eight cents with a frown. Hopefully, this will be enough.

I wait at the bus stop for a few minutes, taking all the Bahamas in. People laughing, talking, having fun, sun shining, palm trees swaying, the smell of ocean water and something sweet hanging in the air. I let out the breath that I didn't realize I was holding. Something feels different than usual, like I don't belong or something. Maybe it's just because I'm alone.

The bus pulls up, and I'm the only one at the stop, so I get on. I hand him my money, and he takes it all, leaving me no change. That's the perfect amount I guess! I walk down the aisle and sit in the open seat on the left.

Just now, I'm realizing that Ben is a fugitive. Everyone has forgotten about the real fugitive: Conner Wills. My mind goes in all sorts of directions, thinking way too much for me to handle. Right now, it hits me hard that I'm a *missing kid* off in the middle of Nassau, Bahamas *by myself*. I start to panic. At first, it's just in my head, but then it's hard for me to breathe. The man across the aisle is smoking, and that's not helping one bit. He looks at me like I'm crazy.

I sink down in my seat and try to think happy thoughts. A glimpse of a large building makes me feel much better. *Historic Museum of the Lost Rennald Ship*. Springing from my seat, I nearly bump my head on the low ceiling. The last name rings out in my memory; it's Christopher's and Maria's last name!

I dash to the front of the bus. "Stop! Stop the bus!" I yell and run off while it's still stopping.

I stumble down the bus steps and find myself in front of the place Ben will be: a large museum with a ship statue out front. I turn around to thank the bus driver, but I see only a poster attached to the back of the bus as it's driving away. *Take a ride through paradise! Only $3.50 a person!* it reads. Hey, that guy stole my money!

CHAPTER 33

COMING, GOING

Kim

Oliver playfully pushes me into the water. Not that I'm not already wet. I just love it here. The water is so clear, I can see my feet, and I spotted a turtle earlier. We've been "snorkeling" around for about an hour. Oliver calls it snorkeling because we saw the turtle. I really think he's coming out of his shell! Get it? I laugh at the face Oliver makes when he sees a pig walking on the beach.

Then, Henry runs down to us. "I don't mean to intrude on the fun you guys are having, but this is really really bad." He turns his phone towards us, and a news report plays. As soon as it ends, we're all stunned with our mouths hanging open.

"How?" I mutter.

"Conner literally broke out of jail the day he got in and now they're suspecting *Ben* for kidnapping...or even worse...*killing* us?" Hannah asks. "We should have maybe tried to call our parents so they didn't worry, set all this straight " Hannah bites her lip.

"Everyone has forgotten about Conner, and they're after Ben instead. It's all backwards," Lucas whispers. "And we've been too busy treasure hunting and trying to stay alive to use Audrey's phone to call anyone!" he adds.

"Yeah, I already knew all of that. But Audrey is off by herself trying to find Ben," Henry says worriedly, glancing toward town.

"Well, let's go then!" I say, running up on the shore. The others follow, and I grab a towel and slide on my sandals.

"Kim, hurry!" Celia yells down to me from the bustling streets of Nassau. I drop the towel and head up to the bus stop with the others.

"How much money do we have for the bus?" Henry asks. I pull out my two bucks, and together we manage to get nineteen dollars and seventy two cents.

"That's not enough for all of us," Oliver says.

"The sign says three fifty a person, so who's walking?" Lucas asks.

"I volunteer. I did cross country running last summer if we need to run," I tell them, not knowing what I'm getting myself into. Everyone is saying "not it" with their fingers on their noses like kids.

"I guess I will too." Oliver shrugs.

"It's settled then. Oliver and Kim are going to find other transportation," Hannah says, sentimentally looking at Oliver and me.

"Bye! See you at the museum," I say, waving over my shoulder.

"How are we supposed to get there?" Oliver asks.

"Maybe rental bikes or something?" I suggest and look around for something, anything.

"I thought I saw a local park back by the market."

"Let's check there," I say as we start to run in that direction.

We get there minutes later to find a rack of bright blue and yellow bikes up for rent: 20 cents for twenty minutes. "Sounds like a great deal to me, but where are we gonna get the money?" I ask.

"Well, let's look on the street. It usually has some change lying around here and there." I nod, and we check the streets until I start to give up and walk back to the bike rack. I notice a glint of something shiny inside of a drainage hole in the road.

"There!" I yell and run up to the nasty-smelling hole. I lay down next to it and reach my hand in. When I pull it back out, two rusted, smelly quarters are in the palm of my hand. I smile, and we run over to the bikes and put the two quarters in the machine. The bikes unlock, and we hurry to bike to the Rennald's Museum of Sunken Ships.

When we get there, I see what looks like Celia's blonde hair in the window of the museum on the second floor. We rush in the sliding doors and up the stairs, past a giant boat model. Along the stairs are mannequins lined up encased in glass. They all are wearing ragged clothes and wooden shoes. They look realistic, like if I wasn't paying any attention, I would think they're real.

All except for one at the very top of the stairs. A gold plate is there underneath a sculpture, with the words *Christopher Rennald, 1632 to 1668*. I stand there looking at his statue for a long time. Our "ghost," the journal's writer, Celia's friend and maybe even crush from the time traveling…Christopher.

"Kim, come on!" Oliver calls.

"Coming," I mutter and take one last look at the captain's hat Christopher's statue is wearing. When I walk up the last few steps and walk over to Oliver, we see Ben. He's laying on the ground, handcuffed.

CHAPTER 34

ALL ALONE

Hannah

It all happened too fast. As soon as we got to the museum, the police were pulling in, looking for Ben because he was last seen here. We tried to cover for him and tell the police the truth, that this is all a misunderstanding, but it's useless at this point. The police are speaking some sort of Spanish and gesturing for us to go downstairs. We do as we're told and start walking downstairs.

"What do we do now?" I whisper. "I mean, we have less than five minutes until we're taken to jail, and it all goes downhill from there."

We walk in silence until Audrey breaks it. "Hannah, do you still have your key?" She looks at me, pushing her brown, frizzy hair behind her ear. I nod.

"Can I use it?" she asks.

I nod again, handing her the key. While the police are distracted with Ben upstairs and speaking more Spanish to him that he says he can't understand, she runs over to the case with the gold plate in it and unlocks the glass door to it. I tiptoe inside the glass door into a long, slanting hallway that has many mannequins in a row.

"Find a mannequin and take all the clothes off," Audrey says, removing the shoes from one. I walk over to a tall mannequin and remove the outfit. The dusty clothes of a maiden are on the floor beside me, and an empty mannequin is pushed out of sight.

"Now, put on the mannequin's clothes," Audrey says, and all of our eyes widen.

"Hurry! We can't have more than two minutes until the police and Ben come down these stairs," she commands while putting on the ragged sailor outfit. We all let out small laughs once we're dressed in our mannequin clothes. Luckily, I chose the maiden dress while I could.

"Now, go in the place of the mannequin and don't move–no matter what. The cops won't take us then," Audrey says, freezing in place on the platform the mannequin was on. When she finishes her sentence, I hear one of the cops let out an angry shout in Spanish.

We all do the same thing as Audrey, and I don't blink for so long, my eyes start to water. I physically can't breathe either, with how tight this dress is. My lungs feel like they're being drained of air when finally the cops and Ben come down the stairs. The four male officers don't even notice us. They're all too busy with making phone calls and yanking Ben down the steps. When Ben passes me, he gives a small smile and a wink. I barely smile back because I don't want to give away the trick.

As soon as I hear the museum doors close, I let out a gigantic breath. I hobble over to Celia and nudge her to untie my dress. She unties the corset. Instant relief. I can breathe again.

"Thanks! That is so much better," I tell her.

"Yeah, no problem, but where do we go now? The police are after us," Celia says, walking out of the mannequin hall and back up to the second floor of the museum.

We follow her quickly. I walk over to a big window in the center of the wall, past the museum models, pictures, and exhibits. The police cars are gone in the parking lot.

"It's all clear. We can go," Lucas says, and we run back downstairs and out the doors.

"Where are we going? We obviously have to look for clues, but I'm starving. We didn't eat lunch, and it's almost eight o'clock," Oliver says, pulling a little watch out of his pouch.

"Well, I guess we can eat dinner and then go back to looking for the treasure," I suggest.

"Food? Ben is in jail right now and you're thinking about treasure and dinner?" Kim is clearly very annoyed with me.

"He smiled and winked at me when he was being pulled down the stairs. Ben won't go to prison until court is over, and he'll spend a night or two locked up at the most," I explain as some of them look confused about how I know all of this. "What? I watch a lot of mystery movies. This is what he wanted all his life: to find the treasure. We can't let Ben's lifelong mission go to waste now! We have to keep looking. And we can't find any clues if we're all starving and collapse from hunger," I finish. The others nod in agreement.

"Maybe we can get a bite to eat there." Lucas points to a small diner across the road.

"Alright," I say, and we walk over to the restaurant.

Kim opens the door, and a little bell rings above the entrance. The restaurant has a homey feel and has pretty fairy lights on the ceiling. We all sit down in a booth, and a smiling waitress walks over.

"Hi, welcome to Caliste's Diner. I'm Caliste, and I'll be your server," the young woman says in an accent that's hard to make out. She reminds me of Michelle, the cabin counselor.

"We'll have one large jelly-filled donut please," Lucas says, after we discuss what we can afford with only two bucks.

"Alright! And that'll be it?" Caliste asks, scribbling our order down on her notepad.

"Yes," I say.

"Ok, what do we do after this?" Celia asks in a hushed tone.

"We look for something that would tell us what direction the treasure is. I mean, it would have to be washed up somewhere, and the ship museum didn't have answers to the treasure, not that we had a lot of time to look," I say.

"I saw one section about treasure, but it was just about treasure hunters and some underwater ships. I read it; many ships could have treasure at sea, but that's all it said," Lucas says.

We've lost Ben and don't have leads, I think. Great.

Oliver speaks up suddenly. "You know what I just thought of? The ghost that we thought was real, it was Conner the whole time!

CHAPTER 35

NEW ANSWERS

Oliver

"It all makes sense now," I say.

"What all makes sense?! I'm so lost," Kim says, her eyes wide.

"Ok, ok, let's go back to when we gave Crow the gold box we got from the caves. I think Conner was spying on us while we did that. This was his master plan. Conner planned to follow us around after he broke out of jail. He scared Dr. Crow out of his mind by sneaking into his house while he was at the pawn shop and writing *'return what you've taken to where it belongs'* on his mirror." I gesture wildly with my hands. "And Conner was *trying* to get him to put the gold box back in the ground where we found it, but Crow is loopy enough to think he meant to return that candy bar he stole as a kid!"

I continue, "So then, when we drove away, Conner was waiting to cut down that tree at the exact moment when we would talk about ghosts. Same with the wasp incident. He could've pushed a beehive over or something because there's no way hundreds of wasps would come out of nowhere and sting you. Now, Conner is just waiting patiently for us to find the treasure and return it to

Christopher's grave so he can unbury it and have it for himself! That's just a guess," I finish, and six astonished faces stare at me.

"How did you think of that?!" Lucas says a little too loudly.

Caliste comes over with a plate and a jelly donut the size of my head. "Enjoy!" she says. We thank her, and everyone turns back to me.

"So?" Hannah and Audrey ask in unison.

"It just came to me suddenly. All of it fits together like a puzzle. We were just missing some pieces," I say and take a delicious bite of the jelly donut.

"So now we just have to find the treasure and pretend to bury it in Christopher's grave. Then, when Conner starts to strike and unbury it, we take him to the cops. Easy enough," Henry says. We all laugh.

I turn to face Henry, but behind him, on the wall, I see something unusual. A colorful mural. "Guys, what's that?" I ask.

"It looks like a compass of some kind. And a…a yellow flower," Hannah says. I nod and start exploring around the mural map on the wall.

"It's an entire map of the island!" Kim says, reading my mind.

"Look over there—on that side of the wall—the Bermuda Triangle!" Lucas says, walking over to it. He drags his finger across the wall from the tip of the Triangle facing the island all the way to a shoreline directly south of us. "I think we just got ourselves a treasure," Lucas says.

The little bell above the door jingles as a strangely familiar girl steps into the diner. "It's good to be back," she says.

Hannah freezes, and her face goes white like she's seen a ghost. *"Catherine?"* she whispers.

Chapter 36

Back Again

Catherine

I stand on the same wooden floor of Christopher's house and watch as something I never believed would have happened takes place in front of my eyes. In the bedroom, the journal I've had for years comes alive, shaking across my desk after that Celia girl I spotted traveled back inside the pages.

Now, white and gold swirls of color illuminate the dim cottage. A portal appears out of the journal, and I take a step back, astonished this is *finally* happening. My eyes grow wide as a mystical wind leaves me hurtling toward the gap in time. The warmth of the journal's pages pull me in, and I feel as light as a feather. The familiar ocean tides sensation washes over me as I fall.

When Celia found the journal Christopher hid in that wooden crate behind the painting and went back to her time, it stayed open just long enough for me to go through, I realize. I've waited for this moment for *67 years. That means I'm 78 years old. It hasn't felt that long, but it's true.* From the time I entered this timeline, I've dreamed of all that's gone on since I left. In the 1600's, almost nothing was invented yet. Everything I've ever known in my daily 1955 life was missing. I especially missed my friends and family.

Through the journal pages, I can see a long, winding road lined with palm trees starting to form below me. As I keep falling through the pages and time, I think that I'll miss Christopher and my daughter, but I need to go back. I love them, but I was never supposed to be in their time. Everything was a mistake, and I never got the chance to tell Christopher the truth of where I came from; now he's gone, I think.

Dropping down from the journal's portal into the sunny, palm tree land, my feet touch the road at last, and a loud honking makes me jump out of the way. A car swerves around me. "Watch where you're going, little girl!" a man yells out of the car window.

Little girl? Where am I?

CHAPTER 37

TIME HAS PASSED

Hannah

"How do you possibly know my name? Wait…I'm…" Catherine pauses and catches her reflection in the glass door, "eleven again?"

"I know your name because you're the top missing person of 1955! I…I actually saw pieces of your lost memories at camp." Everyone's eyes widen. "I'm guessing when you were trapped in the journal, even though you were gone for almost seventy years, you changed back to how you were when you left!" I'm talking quickly because this is so amazing. "Now you're back, and you're the same age as when you left–just like Celia went through almost forty years of Christopher's life and didn't age at all when she returned. Also how *did* you manage to get trapped in the journal?" I ask, a little out of breath.

"There was a *real* ghost of Catherine at camp?" Oliver clarifies. "But just saying my ideas about Conner are still right I think."

"Yeah, Catherine's ghost—or memories—didn't do those things. I saw her the first night at camp. Then her ghost led me to

Ben's basement." Hannah bites her lip. "I didn't want to say anything because I didn't even know if she was real or if I was hallucinating or something." She turns to Catherine. "But you're back. You're not a missing person anymore!"

Catherine looks very surprised at all of this. She explains, "I found the journal in a cottage behind a painting and time traveled four hundred years into the past. I met Christopher, and we got married when I was 16; we had Maria, our baby, when I was 19. She was precious. And forty years after that, Christopher died from an assassin who wanted his treasure." Young, little eleven-year-old Catherine sighs, and it feels crazy to me that she got married and then became a little kid again! "I went through Christopher's life, but all the time I was there it was in flashes, scenes. One minute Maria was a newborn baby, the next she was a toddler, then a teenager and looked as old as I was!"

Celia nods like she completely understands, but to be honest, I'm totally lost and think the others are too. "And seventy years felt like a few months. I lived seventy years in maybe a fourth of that time and aged the whole time. Then, the portal that Celia traveled through opened up for me, and I came back here, leaving Maria to her husband and family where she'd be safe." She smiles. "Wow, I get to live two lives, now that I'm young again."

Everyone is processing what Catherine and I said when a news report flashes on the television...with our seven faces in the middle of the screen.

Chapter 38

Runaways

Henry

"Hey, well look at that. It seems we have not one but seven runaways in my very restaurant," Caliste says, smiling kind of freakishly at us.

"Run!" Lucas shouts, and we all book it out of there.

"Oops, forgot the donut," I say, and I run back in the diner and grab the half-eaten pastry.

"Thank you!" I yell to Caliste as I run to catch up to the others.

"What now?!" Audrey asks as we sprint down the street and don't look back.

"We go south!" Catherine shouts, and she gestures toward a tour bus.

"We don't have enough money!" Hannah shouts back. Lucas grins like he's got a plan. Oh boy, please tell me his plan isn't...

"Lucas no," I mutter. But he jumps on the back of the bus.

"It's going south. I saw the schedule of the bus routes!"

"Well okay!" I say and hop on with him. Then Oliver joins us.

"Come on, girls, don't be scaredy-cats!" Oliver says to them, and they all give each other the look that girls give when they think a guy is being dumb.

"Alright," Celia says, rolling her eyes as she sprints and jumps. The others follow her.

"Hang on tight!" I scream as the bus starts moving. We grip onto the metal handles on the back, and the girls all close their eyes. Lucas and Hannah hold hands.

As we speed through town, I look around and realize this is pretty fun! I let out a cheer. Instant regret, I tell you. An old woman whips her head around and sees seven teenagers right in front of her face through the back window of the bus. I would have fainted if I was her too.

"Um…guys, look," Lucas says, tilting his head to the woman on the floor. "Perfect time to jump!" he says and leaps onto the sandy shore.

"Oh great," Oliver says and jumps too. I do the same, and my shoes sink into the sand; some grains gets in my eyes. When I can actually see again, everyone has jumped, except for Kim. Oliver is running after the bus and begging her to jump.

"I can't!" Kim says, visibly shaking. I start to run after Oliver. Luckily, the bus wasn't going too fast, or else we'd be stuck there for a long time. Finally, Kim takes the leap of faith right into Oliver's arms, and they both fall backwards into the sand. I wholeheartedly smile.

When they stand up, Kim kisses Oliver's cheek, and I swear he almost falls back down again. I'm happy for him; I don't think he's ever been kissed by a girl. Other than his mom, no offense bro. We all collect ourselves and join back together on the beach. Oliver is red as a tomato, and he can't stop staring at Kim.

"This is for sure where the treasure is, right Lucas?" I ask him.

"I'm almost positive." He looks determined.

"Christopher told me that the treasure would be in the Bahamas, and I think Lucas has a good instinct," Catherine says, looking up at us and smiling. She's shorter than us all at only 11 years old now.

"Oliver, what do you remember on the wall of the diner that could lead us to the treasure?" Kim asks him.

"What? Sand. Kiss. Yellow," he says, almost in a trance. Kim laughs and rolls her eyes.

"Anyone else remember anything?" I ask.

"Not really. It seemed like a pretty standard map to me," Audrey says.

"Yeah, nothing too special," Hannah agrees. She plays with her necklace.

"Maybe if we just start looking around, we'll find something useful," Lucas says, seeming like he's on his last nerve with this treasure. He's gone through a lot with us, and he can't get this close and not find it. I couldn't bare to see that.

"We're gonna find this treasure if it's the last thing I do," I say and start walking down the shore.

"Wouldn't other people have found it by now? I mean, this isn't the most popular beach ever, but it's definitely been used," Kim says.

"That's a good point," I tell her.

"What are we missing though? There has to be some kind of marking that shows where this flipping treasure is," Lucas says, getting angry. "Everyone think." He paces around the beach, and he's honestly getting me stressed out.

"Now that you mention it, I do remember a flower painted on the wall of the diner. I think it's called a yellow elder," Celia says.

"A yellow elder. Yellow elder." Audrey types the words into her phone.

"It says they grow all over the Bahamas. That has to be where the treasure is. Somewhere near this flower," she says, showing her phone screen to us.

Lucas is long gone, way over by a rocky area along the ocean. I shout at the top of my lungs, "Lucas! We have a clue!"

CHAPTER 39

WORTH THE WAIT

Lucas

I swear my heart skips a hundred beats at once when I hear those words come out of Henry's mouth. "It's about time!" I yell and start running toward them.

"Where is it? What clue?" I ask impatiently.

"Near or under yellow elders," Celia explains.

"What the heck is a yellow elder?"

"A flower, genius," Hannah says, laughing.

I check the flower photo and nod. "So let's start looking!" I say. I speed-walk the shore line, going up and down the beach for ages as the tides flow. I'm way too impatient at this point.

"Come on, where are these yellow elders?" Audrey asks. A second later, a glimpse of green bushes in the distance catches my attention.

"Maybe over there?" I suggest and start to sprint. We arrive at the bushes and see nothing but leaves, no flowers in sight. "Great, just amazing," I say sarcastically, sitting down on a rock. I bury my face in my hands and feel the hope draining from me. We went through all of this for nothing.

Someone taps my shoulder. "Lucas," Hannah says, and she points to one tiny golden yellow elder on the bush. I jump to my feet and sweep Hannah off hers. I hear the others' screams, but all I see is that one precious flower.

"Well?" Hannah asks, smiling ear to ear. "There's nothing left to do but dig!" She pushes the big bush's leaves aside to look under it.

Under all of the greenness, something in the sand leaves my stomach upside down. It's a little concrete plate with an engraved heart in it and a tinier heart inside it. Hannah silently lifts the locket we found in the journal from her neck. Catherine gasps and says, "That's Christopher's locket! He told me it was family jewelry passed down." Hannah smiles and presses the gold locket heart to the concrete one. It fits perfectly! The locket splits into seven pieces.

Hannah hands one piece to each of us, a new gold chain appearing in my hand. I start to attach the piece of the heart to the chain, but it magically melts together, forming a necklace. I'm astonished, thinking this is literally meant to be. I'm almost to the maximum of amazement I can handle when I look down at my piece and see my name etched into the side of it. *Lucas*. All our jaws drop to the ground. I'm about to speak, but some things are left unexplained, like Ben told us before. I clip the locket sliver around my neck.

When I lift the concrete plate off the ground, it's heavier than it seems. Under the plate is a big, oak wood chest with two gold handles just waiting to be opened.

"This is it," I whisper. "One. Two. Three." We all pull the chest out of the ground and do the same for eleven others after that.

Holy mother of gold! We open every chest, and each one has a different gift inside. Gold, diamonds, rubies, emeralds, jewelry. It all seems like a dream.

When I look up from the treasure, reality slaps me in the face…because a shadow of Conner Wills lurks behind a fence about thirty feet away.

"Guys, we have to return this to where it belongs, to Christopher's grave up the shore, right?" I say forcefully, and I wink at the others.

Catherine nods, *"Yes, that's right. We don't want to make the ghost mad!"* she says, and we start lugging the chests one by one and digging separate holes for each. We use a strip of driftwood for the "tombstone."

Kim takes the gold plate with Christopher's name on it that she stole from the museum and props it up on the wood.

"*Good work guys. Let's go home,*" Oliver says, and we start walking away, smiling at each other.

Audrey dials 911 while we all hide behind a shed near the beach. We can see the fake grave from our view, and Conner starts to dig into the sand with his hands. The police answer Audrey's call, and we explain our problem. Luckily, the police officer speaks great English. She ends the call and says, "The cops will be here in less than five minutes."

"When they get here, we stay in hiding until they bring Conner to the police car, and then we get our treasure, clear Ben's name, and finally head home," Kim adds. I nod at the plan, and we wait until we hear the police cars pull up. The officers get out and run down to Conner, who cusses loudly.

"Ok, any second they'll be taking him to jail," Celia says anxiously. The police handcuff Conner, put him in the car, and pull out of the beach's parking lot. We wait till we can't hear sirens anymore.

Then Audrey's phone rings. "Who is it?" I ask her.

Audrey's hazel eyes meet mine, her gaze worried. "It's Ben."

CHAPTER 40

THE BIG CHOICE

Audrey

"Answer!" Henry says frantically. I click the answer button, and Ben's face appears on the screen via FaceTime video chat.

"Ben! Are you in jail?" I ask.

"No, no, I'm not, and I'm not going to be either. I'm clear of all charges, and I'm going to be back at my shop soon enough! I told the police everything about Conner, and when they looked at his records, they believed me." He grins. "My friend from Rhode Island is coming to the Bahamas on summer vacation and will drive his boat home then. You kids don't worry about me! I also called and explained everything to your parents and the camp. Stay at the hotel tonight; it's still paid for through tomorrow, and your parents are going to come get you in the morning," he says, smiling.

"That's amazing! Guess what? We found the treasure!" Lucas says excitedly.

"I knew you had it in you!" Ben exclaims. Lucas blushes, and Hannah squeezes his hand.

"Well, go get it kids, and do what your gut tells you to do with it," Ben says and waves goodbye. I let out a gigantic sigh of relief.

"He's ok," I say and lean back on the rusty shed.

"Now what?" Henry asks.

"We go with our gut," Kim says, and we all laugh.

Just then, my piece of the locket lifts off my chest and pulls me toward the ocean. The chain rubs hard against the back of my neck. "What the heck?!" I shout because I don't know what to think. Soon, everyone else's lockets are doing the same thing.

"How is this happening?" Lucas asks, his face drained of color.

When my feet hit the water, the locket lightly drops back down to my chest.

"I think the locket wants us to put the treasure in the water," Hannah mutters beside me.

"No no no! There's no way I'm putting millions of dollars into the water," Lucas says stiffly.

"The locket made its decision," Henry says, shrugging, eyes wide as the jewels in the treasure.

"So we're bringing it out to sea?" I ask.

"It feels right," Kim says.

"This is insane!" Lucas says, but then he smiles. "I kind of like it." We all laugh at him and then realize seven magic necklaces are trying to tell us something. And we're listening.

CHAPTER 41

LAST GOODBYE

Hannah

"You guys know what I just realized?" I ask. They all shake their heads. "Ben's grandma, the one who found the bottle with the map piece, her last name was Rennald." Kim tilts her head at me, confused.

"As in Christopher Rennald's great great great great granddaughter?!" Oliver says, and my locket hops a little. A wall of realization comes crashing down.

"Oh my goodness, you're right! Ben is related to Christopher!" Kim says. I nod, and we all sit there in silence for a minute with the ocean waves whispering.

"We need to find the shipwreck! The Rennald shipwreck would be straight ahead of us, according to the map of the island!" Catherine says, and she walks back to the fake grave.

"Let's unbury these chests," Celia says, and we all start to dig with our hands. Before long, we have all twelve chests out, and we each grab one to drag into the ocean. We walk with our treasure out to sea, and the drop off isn't for a while, so we can all touch the sand–except for little Catherine.

The sun is almost set, and the fluffy clouds float above the pink sky and blue water. I walk through the waves for a long time with the chest I'm gripping onto. Finally, I can't touch the ocean's sandy floor anymore; there's an immediate drop off after that.

I put my head underwater and open my eyes. It stings a little, but it's worth it. We all slowly swim down to the very bottom of the ocean, which isn't too far.

Then I see it.

The ship gives me major *Titanic* vibes at first. The lost Rennald ship has been found by seven teenagers and a magical locket possessed by the ghost of Christopher Rennald himself!

We gently set the treasure inside the broken shipwreck and wave goodbye. Then, we all swim back to shore, and my heart beats loudly in my chest. The water shimmers against the stars in the now twilight sky. We all sit back on the shore in victory.

"This has been by far the best adventure I've ever had in my life," Lucas says.

"Definitely," I whisper and lay my head on his shoulder. I set my hand on the sand, but I feel something sharp. I look down, and a big, broken piece of seaglass is laying beside me. I nudge Lucas, and his eyes widen, his mouth falling open. The sea glass has fogged up, and written in the same neat cursive from in the journal is:

Thank You

ABOUT THE AUTHOR

Grace Manderfeld is a new author with a passion for writing and reading. She published her first novelette, *Snow Days*, at age 10 and now her first novella, *Into the Forest*, at age 12. Grace enjoys dance, painting, and spending time with family, friends, and her dog Penny.

CPSIA information can be obtained
at www.ICGtesting.com
Printed in the USA
JSHW061559281222
35443JS00004B/21